THE

PARATROOPER

OF

MECHANIC

AVENUE

BY LESTER GORAN

the

paratrooper

of

mechanic

avenue

HOUGHTON MIFFLIN COMPANY BOSTON
THE RIVERSIDE PRESS CAMBRIDGE · 1960

c. 2

First Printing

The Riverside Press
Cambridge, Massachusetts
Printed in the U.S.A.

H R

SEP 7 '60

FOR DEEDEE WHO BELIEVED

THE

PARATROOPER

OF

MECHANIC

AVENUE

A small segment of American life describ-
ed with painful fidelity. The story centers
around Isaac born in a Pittsburgh tenement
among the downtrodden.

1

Ike-o Hartwell was born in the cold winter of 1931. It
happened unexpectedly in the toilet room on the second
floor of the tenement at 432 Gardenia Street.

His mother was an uncomplicated woman. She weighed
more than two hundred pounds under normal conditions
and this weight climbed even higher during her pregnancy.
She was a quiet, lonely woman; she became easily confused with the simplest discussions. She did not understand anything until it was explained to her many times.
Until her marriage to the Protestant Hartwell she had been
deeply religious. She still believed at the time of her pregnancy that there would be some divine sign heralding the
approach of childbirth. There was no one on Gardenia
Street or in the whole of Sobaski's Stairway either to tell
her differently.

She rose from her straight-backed kitchen chair at the
fourth-floor window only to go down to the communal
toilet on the second floor or to cut another triangle of black

bread and spread out on it thick layers of ketchup or mayonnaise. About the time darkness came she would tire of sitting and move back from the scarred window sill to lick the day's encrusted food from her callused little fingers. Yolanda seldom washed because of her lethargic temperament and the high price of soap. She tended herself like an overgrown oblivious cat, startled out of her reveries by only the most direct assaults, a car horn, a burst of profanity from the street below, or a sudden impetuous sharp slap to her cheek from Charlie to rouse her.

Sometimes she kept a knife, a loaf of the black bread, and two bottles of seasoning at her chair so as to avoid having to stand to get them. She claimed that sound European country blood had been weakened by climbing American city stairs and had sent to early graves every member of her large family before they were forty years old. She thought that any unnecessary movement would hasten the blood disease in her.

She believed that the recent unfamiliar aches in her arms and legs were the beginning of her family's ailments; she did not know herself that she was pregnant until her seventh month. When she told Charlie he looked directly into her impassive eyes, and said, "I don't believe you, but take some castor oil anyhow. There's a lot of things Charlie don't want right now, and, sister, a baby is one of them."

She went to kiss him, but he pushed her away. Like the photograph of her own Stanachek mother and father in the dark egg-shaped print over the mantel, she was stocky and thick limbed with humped sloping shoulders and a broad undefined bust. He found her repulsive.

They had been married for fifteen years at that time; and Charlie thought over her announcement for a few days and decided he needed a drink. He disappeared for a week and came staggering home on a Friday night, chin red-stubbled and smelling of vomit, and went to sit on the bed but fell heavily to the floor instead. "Goddamn it, Yolanda, it's six o'clock, where's supper?" he croaked. He fell asleep on the floor while she hurried to prepare the food.

The days were low and gray the winter Ike-o was born; the cold seemed to come up from the bottom of the frozen Chartier's Creek that February. Charlie sat bundled in a blanket in the sunless back room at DeAngelo's when he was not home. He drank 120-proof white lightning with Thaddeus Smolcher, and the two of them passed away the winter nights counting out for each other their hundreds of accumulated hatreds.

Fats Smolcher had bought a small Ford and posted circus and theater signs for a ticket distributing company. He admired Charlie and always had a dollar bill in his pocket for him. He was at that time the father of five children. For the most part his wife did not allow him in the house until she was safely asleep with her door locked; he drank with Charlie until dawn lit up the rust-gray Sobaski's Stairway sky, then would go down to Sixth Street, crank up his Ford and go out with a long handled brush to plaster up bright spangled posters on poles and building sides.

In the nighttime of DeAngelo's back room Charlie was listened to with great respect. He had an opinion on every subject under the sun for the loafers and jobless who congregated there on weekdays to avoid the wind. The drunker he became the more he swayed in his chair and the more profound he seemed to himself. He basked in the mute praises given him by the crew in DeAngelo's back room and resented every minute he was forced to be under the roof at 432 Gardenia Street.

Yolanda complained to him about the pains in her arms and legs and said the cold made them worse.

"You ever make a move to clean up this pigpen you might stir up your circulation," he said. "There ain't a louse in Sobaski's Stairway don't got the courage to point their finger at my back and say, 'There goes the man was dumb enough to marry a hog.'"

At Charlie Hartwell's core was a love and hatred for the neighborhood in which he had been born. He loved it as he loved himself and hated the flaking, decaying slum in equal measure. There was nothing that occurred in Sobaski's Stairway that he did not receive as something directed at himself. The recent immigrations of Polish, the Jews and Italians and Syrians, then the Negroes, he accepted as a personal insult to himself, to his family history in the neighborhood.

The twisting slum of small wooden frame houses, cobblestoned alleys, speak-easies, brothels, and brown tenements, sneaking around and converging on Mechanic Avenue, was the particular place meant by most outsiders when they spoke of Sobaski's Stairway. The famous landmark, a rendezvous for a generation of bootleggers, was at Fifteenth Street where the slum ended and the worked-out mounds began.

Sobaski, the carpenter, had built the stairs himself up
Harris' Hill. He found moonshining more to his liking than
carpentry or coal mining; his fame, for all of his invisibility,
touched the entire collection of buildings once known as
Greendale, and invested them with his mood of mischief
and suspicion, as well as his name. He was seen infre-
quently, but it was known that he crouched all night long
and Sunday afternoon in the thick foliage on the slope of
Harris' Hill. For most of his customers he was never more
than a hand, a gun barrel, a greenhorn's raspy voice in
the night. "Sure t'ing, my friend," he would say when he
was positive money had been left for him on the second
landing.

When Charlie squinted his eyes he could see from the
undergrowth emerge a brightly labeled bottle, pushed out
onto the first landing by Sobaski's big miner's hand. He
had grown up with Metro Sobaski, but the tilted shotgun
barrel was not withdrawn into the brush until the miner's
hand scooped in the money placed before it on the landing. If there was no money forthcoming he usually said,
"No money, no sure t'ing moonshine, go home my friend,
get offen my steps." It was said that he kept his gun
trained on the back of a person's head all the long, sad
march downward.

The Sunday night Ike-o was born Charlie Hartwell had
climbed the stairs empty-handed with nothing but the
biggest thirst in the universe for a companion.

"I'll pay you when I got it," he pleaded with the unseen
gun, "just push one of them Johnny's Choice pints out
here, Metro — you know how it is with me. Yolanda is

expecting and I haven't been doing too good. You know Charlie Hartwell is good for it when he got it."

"Please, my friend, don't block the goddamn stairway, if you please."

"Ungrateful hunky," Charlie mumbled, numb but still sober.

He walked down the stairway, thinking that he would drink iodine if someone gave it to him at a price he could afford. That would be the fast twenty-three cents in his pocket, two dimes and three pennies. He shook off the feeling the steps gave him. He paused to let another man pass him going up. He looked eagerly into the man's face, but was disappointed to see he was a Negro. "Buddy," Charlie said, "I need fifty cents real bad. What do you say? Help a fellow human being in trouble."

The man did not turn.

Charlie looked down and thought of the baby, Yolanda, and his thirst. Fifteenth Street seemed friendly below, and before Sobaski had built the stairway Charlie had played on Harris' Hill and wondered how it would be to have wings and fly as the pigeons and starlings did. He tried to shake off the feeling. There was no guarantee that things would be better if he did jump.

The steps lay night and day as unchangeable as Harris' Hill itself. Mothers told their children that angels had built the steps, and, on moonlit nights with every picket and step illuminated in silver, any other explanation would have seemed a falsehood. "A person can't pray around this place without thinking of them steps," was once a saying in Sobaski's Stairway. There twisted upward an answer to prayers and a solution to the pains of mortality; it wound through the scrub brush and dogwood and needed paint by daylight but was silver by the full moon and forever was high, high enough to be lethal. Charlie stood shivering and sober in the dark wind and, looking down at the rooftops below, he thought that it would be old Charlie's luck to fall in a freak way that would leave him in pain for forty years before he died. He walked the cobblestones to Gardenia Street slowly. He walked in the middle of the streets because the black doorways might contain anything. He walked with his eyes down. He had nowhere to go but home.

His thirst was as tall as he was and more the man. It walked alone and was the only real life in the wind-weary February night.

He came into his apartment and went to the kitchen chair and sat. He was too grave for a fat little man, too gray in his face for his ruddy complexion and sparse reddish hair. He did not look at his wife when she spoke.

"It's going to be soon, Charlie," Yolanda said again, but louder.

"I don't get no peace no matter where I go," Charlie said. "I might as well be sitting in a speak as coming home here to listen to you."

He was only an inch taller than Yolanda, but he seemed to draw himself to a great height when he stood. He held his paunch in like a cat putting up its back, more to frighten than for a use in combat. "How would you like a punch in your hunky kisser?" he asked. "Would that get the idea across to you I got things on my mind I don't want you interrupting?"

She saw he was not drunk and pitied him even more.

She became sad for him when he shouted, and she cried with him at night when some unimaginable thing woke him and made him weep. She had held him long nights trying to draw into herself that anger that was in her husband, but even her big arms enfolding him had not been enough. She pitied him most when he drew himself up this way and swelled angrily and only a fool would not know it was his humiliation and fear that did it to him.

They had been married for fifteen years, and Yolanda thought she understood him less with each year.

"You be hitting two people tonight, honeybunch, you take a swing at me," she said. "The baby, he ain't done nothing to you."

Charlie Hartwell did not know the sound of kindness; he did not hear it in Yolanda's voice.

"You going to give me some peace," he cried, "or do I got to walk out on you. Now, watch yourself, you're forcing me into something I don't want to do."

They both knew he would not be there if he had the price of a pint.

"Charlie, you don't want to be walking around tonight without an overcoat," she said. "How come you don't sit over there by the light and write Governor Pinchot a letter like you said you was going to do? I think it's a damn shame people don't put out the American flag like they used to when we was kids."

"The country went to the lice," he said. "I'd burn the governor's ear good I ever put down on paper what I got on my mind about how they do disrespect to Washington every time his birthday comes up. I didn't see more than one or two flags all day. When I was a kid a person would be run out of town they didn't show their colors February twenty-second."

Yolanda smiled proudly.

"You write a fine letter, Charlie," she said.

She was pleased with the sudden glow in his face; he wasn't so bad, she thought, when he wasn't drinking.

He went to the kitchen table and opened a drawer and took out a fountain pen. "I bet you think I'm afraid to tell the governor he ain't no better than these lice he don't make it illegal not to display the flag today," he said.

"I think no such thing, honeybunch, I know there ain't nothing or nobody my Charlie is afraid of," she said.

He nodded as he listened to her. His grimness left him, and he became only a little fat man with freckles and a complexion as variable as buttermilk. He pursed his small lips judiciously as he held the fountain pen up to the light and studied it. He knew that Yolanda tried to placate him and felt a sorrow for her as well as himself. A drink would have made someone else out of him tonight: maybe a person who could kiss her and tell her, honey, everything's going to be all right like it once was. But what of her sitting there on the bed with the dull eyes of a cow? He wished a train would hit her or she'd fall out of the window, anything to change that welcome-mat face. She's nine months gone, he thought, and she don't look five pounds bigger than usual. He had not pulled her to him for the past eight years once without the taste of Sobaski's moonshine in his throat. He often felt like punching her.

He put the pen back in the kitchen table. Tonight

everything seemed useless. The governor would probably never even see his letter.

"Charlie," Yolanda said, "you don't look good. Maybe you better not write that letter tonight. I know how much that thinking on one subject takes out of a mind."

Charlie kicked the table leg and walked to the window. He felt as if he would suffocate. He looked out across the street to the rows of windows there. He wondered what happened behind the blinds of someone else's window. Were there a man and a woman happy somewhere? He made himself look away from the windows and felt alone because he had nowhere else to sit that was warm and not the price of a pint in his pocket.

Yolanda laughed anxiously. She wondered what mood had seized him now. "Charlie, honey, you should have been a lawyer the way you handle the language," she said, and waited hopefully. She hoped he would warm to her kindness. But he did not turn from the window.

His reputation as a lawyer had come because he was able to fill in at least half of the crossword puzzles in the paper. Yolanda didn't know one word; she believed that Charlie Hartwell was some kind of genius. She did not tell him but she wanted the baby and desired that it should be like its father. She would raise him, if it were a boy, not to drink. Charlie now, he might have been a senator if he hadn't a weakness for the bottle.

"Saying our kid is a boy, Charlie, do you think it might be a good-luck sign to have him born on Washington's birthday?"

"No reason not."

Her face was laughable to him: it was serious and dumb and it believed everything. But he did not laugh. He wanted a drink. He went to the icebox and pulled open the wooden door. "How come there ain't anything in here?" he asked. "I put a bottle of ice water in there this morning."

"The ice melted, and I didn't have a quarter for any more. I put our stuff by Rosie Plotkin on the first floor."

"If I put a fist in your eye you'll learn to keep away from them Jews," he said, and turned up the radio. "I don't know why you can't give me peace just one day. If it ain't one thing it's another."

He went to the bed and threw himself into it. He lay diagonally with his shoes on; he wanted her to sleep elsewhere but supposed he'd have to move when she was ready to sleep.

"Charlie, you sleeping?"

"Yeah, I'm sleeping, don't bother me."

"I heard on the radio today Al Capone is going to open up soup kitchens in Chicago. What do you think of that? The papers make him out to be so bad, and I'll bet you he has a heart of gold."

He turned his back to her, and she waited until she was sure he slept before she went over to the bed. She took off his shoes gently and massaged his feet. She pushed him aside without rousing him, and, slowly, because it was difficult to recline at all, she settled herself. She listened to him breathing and rested her hands on her abdomen. In an hour's time she knew that whatever was going to happen was beginning.

"I got cramps again or something else, Charlie," Yolanda said. "Charlie? You sleeping?"

She had complained of pains in her abdomen before. He thought he knew her eating habits too well to be concerned, and when she sat up in bed about one o'clock in the morning he did not stir. He breathed evenly to deceive her. He was morose with his thirst.

"Charlie," she said louder, "I got a different kind of pain, it's like something grabbing me there."

He could hear her gasping in the darkness.

"You ate thirty-four cents' worth of black bread today," he said. "It's talking back to you."

He wanted to put the reality of the baby off even ten minutes if he could. Maybe it was the black bread.

"I think I might be going to have the baby soon, Charlie."

They each heard the other's breathing.

"I say you ain't."

"I better call Rosie Plotkin," Yolanda said. "I better go down to the first floor and call Rosie Plotkin."

"Now, listen, you go to the toilet first. I don't want you waking any of these lice and making a damned fool out of me. Ain't there no time of the day or night I can get some peace — I been laying here all night trying to figure out a way to make a buck, I don't want you intruding."

He felt his voice in his throat and wanted a swallow, a taste, just a taste of something good. He knew no more about babies than Yolanda. What did it mean to have a baby? He was frightened and his throat was dry.

"I don't want to see any of those faces from downstairs

in my home," he said. "I don't want them up here looking at me. You do your business, if your time come, down there."

He heard her groan as she stood.

"Charlie," she said at the door, "I want the baby, saying it's a boy, to be just like my honeybunch."

He listened to her breathing.

"Look kid," he said, "I don't mean half of what I say. You know if you need me Charlie will be there. If this is it, then let me know first."

"I got love for you, Charlie, honest to God. I love you like when we first got married."

He turned away from her, and she went in her flat bare feet down to the toilet room on the second floor. The room was shared by the three families on the second, the three families on the third, and the three on the fourth. On the first floor there was a separate bathroom for the three families living there, and under no circumstances were members of the other nine families to use it. The first-floor residents paid three dollars more a month, and, as happened frequently, in one of the apartments on the first floor there dwelled a pair of prostitutes. They complained most about the use of the first-floor toilet.

In the long still corridor Charlie heard his wife's footsteps. He heard her knock at the toilet door on the second floor. After midnight people went to the toilet room to read because the landlord, the Jefferson Real Estate Company, paid the electricity for the two toilets. It was an oversight on their part. The toilets were occupied from darkness until dawn.

He heard her knock a second time and scream. He waited until he heard her again before he slid over to the edge of the bed. It was as much a shout or a moan as the piercing cry of a woman. He rose silently, fearful of the noise in the bedclothes, fearing to disturb the waiting tenement night by a sound of his own. Screams were not uncommon on Gardenia Street, and behind their doors people waited. Charlie knew these screams were for him; he groped in the darkness for his trousers. He thought that with a drink under his belt he would have been able to meet this situation better. It seemed unreal, somehow dirty. And he was ashamed as if caught in a perverse act. He could not assemble Yolanda's stocky image into the tender, sentimental visions he held of motherhood. The bare wooden floor was cold under his feet, and Charlie Hartwell trembled. He hoped he would see no blood.

He pulled up his suspenders and walked as quietly as he could downstairs. He stalled, himself waiting, pretending that the moans were not meant for him.

Down below the neighbors gathered on the landing. Still Charlie stalled and listened. He wanted to push them aside and rush into the street. He wanted a taste, just a taste of something wet on his dry throat. His flaccid face showed little interest in the crowd before the toilet.

"She come down here to do one thing," Rosie Plotkin cried, "and you can trust Yolanda Hartwell she done something else."

The crowd was festive, and Charlie stood with the patience of a man waiting for a parade to pass. He watched from under his eyebrows; he could not rid himself of the feeling he had been caught in a dirty act. Lice, he thought to steady himself, pack of lice.

The neighbors were in nightgowns and underwear tops and poked each other: a collection of people with half faces from the single bulb in the toilet but laughing and pressing forward and one of the whores drunk and staggering and the other dark and serious, moistening her lips. The two men with the prostitutes were the loudest. "I want to give this kid something," one shouted, digging in his pocket. "I want to give this kid something, it ain't every kid can be born in a whorehouse." His girl friend pulled him back into her apartment.

The half faces grinned at Charlie Hartwell.

"Believe me," Rosie Plotkin said, "this ain't the first baby Rosie brought into the world. So? You have to go to college. Honest to God, I almost had to fish this one out — she come down here thinking she had gas pains and, believe me, she was going to have a baby. If Mr. Arboor hadn't been sitting in there figuring out how to overthrow the government this baby would be on his way down the Chartier's Creek."

The neighbors cleared a path for Rosie. She shuffled through them in her nightgown. She was not as tall as another person on the landing. She held in a brown-stained towel the baby and rocked it gently and clucked at it and laughed. "It ain't the first," she cried. "I know this business, believe me."

Charlie backed away from the bundle.

"*Mazeltov*," Rosie hooted, "it's a boy."

"*Mazeltov*," some of the neighbors shouted.

Charlie stood with his arms at his side. He did not raise them toward the baby. A man in a torn undershirt held up his hand for silence. "I feel a responsibility for this baby," he shouted. "If I wasn't in there studying on the john the poor little fellow might not be here. I say let's make up a collection for the baby and not because he was born in a cathouse. We're decent, honest people, and we're comrades of the working class. Let's show the baby what kind of people we are. We didn't choose to live in no whorehouse."

Some of the neighbors left to come back with coins. Others did not return but stayed hidden; they were ashamed they did not have as much as a dime to give the baby.

"Here's the total," the man in the torn undershirt said. "We collected six dollars and thirteen cents." He turned to Charlie. They both stood in the shadows, and a few of the neighbors leaned over the banister toward them to hear better. "Comrade," the speaker said soberly, "I'm giving you this money, generously donated by representatives of the working class, in the fervent hope that this little baby will see the downfall of a corrupt and bloodsucking system."

"Give him the six dollars already, Arboor, don't make a speech," someone called.

"I got things in my heart when I see that baby, comrade," Arboor shouted.

"The baby ain't old enough to sign no petitions, Arboor."

"Brother, I speak the solidarity of the working class," Arboor said, and held up a book. "This one book here got answers for everything that ails you. There's a big day coming, and that baby there is going to be part of it. Our day is done, comrade, we're as extinct as the dinosaur."

"Make a speech, make a speech."

"Arboor! — you stink like a dinosaur."

"Speech, speech."

Mr. Arboor handed Charlie two handfuls of coins and walked into the light from the toilet and through the crowd. He lived on the third floor. "Make a speech, make a speech" followed him.

Mr. Arboor waited until the shouts stopped.

"I have statistics right here," he said, "showing there ain't one person unemployed in the whole Soviet Union. Does it make sense to you that little baby should be born in a whorehouse?"

"Screw, bum."

"Screw, bum, go wipe yourself."

Mr. Arboor was personally unpopular with the neighbors because he invited Negroes into his apartment and sometimes had a man with a guitar come and play loud songs all night. He had no trade, no profession. The rumor was that he had quit medical school in his final year, but that was not true. He had gone only one year to school and had thought he would major in economics but could not understand the graphs and quit to get married. He frequently embarrassed his wife. She wanted him to find work.

Mrs. Arboor pulled him into their apartment and the neighbors heard them quarreling and then there was quiet.

Charlie Hartwell put the coins in his pocket.

"I want to say something right now," he said. "I want

to tell you you're the whitest bunch of people that ever lived. I always say a man's a man if he's Jew, Gentile, white, or black. It don't mean nothing to me that Mr. Arboor is a Syrian and a Communist. I say that even if a man is a mick or a Jew or a hunky. A man's a man."

The neighbors applauded.

"The great day come," Rosie said. "Play Father Coughlin a little quieter next Sunday."

The crowd cleared a path for Yolanda; and Charlie took her by the arm. "Honey," he said, the six dollars in coins in his pocket weighing heavy and good, "things is going to be different now. This baby changed things for us. Everything is going to be all right now." He meant after three fingers of gin, and that was what that gorgeous weight in his pocket could do.

"*Mazeltov*, Yolanda, darling," Rosie Plotkin said.

Yolanda walked up the steps slowly. She held the baby close against her, leaning her huge build toward Charlie. There was an odd solemnity to the two people walking up the stairs. Yolanda and Charlie both wept. "Honest," Charlie mumbled, "things is really going to be different. I ain't been perfect."

"You're all right, Charlie," she said.

Rosie ran downstairs to fetch a Coca-Cola for Yolanda.

In their apartment Charlie paced the floor trying to make a decision. But he could not wait for morning. He put on his socks and shoes, and, having no overcoat, a thick woolen sweater with a basketball emblem and the initial "W" sewn on. It was a sweater he had copped in a speak. He did not look at Yolanda or the baby.

She had placed the baby in an upturned orange crate on a pillow, and she sat happily looking from the baby to Charlie.

"I'll be back in half an hour," Charlie said, still not looking toward the window.

"Take your time, honeybunch, you earned a drink."

Charlie Hartwell passed Rosie on the steps as she ran with the Coca-Cola before her. It was a belief on Gardenia Street that if carbonated drinks were not consumed instantly their potency evaporated with the fizz. The fizz was believed to have a beneficial effect on the upper stomach. So Rosie ran with the bottle up the stairs.

Charlie went directly with the six dollars to Sobaski's stairway and bought two pints. There was only one place in the world he could go. He had a relative, an unmarried cousin known to everyone as Cocky Jones, and this cross-eyed old drunkard lived mostly in a tar-paper shack on a riverbank a mile out of Frugality, Pennsylvania, thirty-eight miles away. Charlie visited him once or twice a year and came home when Cocky took one of his spitting fits or disappeared himself somewhere downstream.

On the occasion of Ike-o's birth Charlie stayed for three weeks. He came home angry and tired and argumentative. He demanded that Yolanda change the baby's name from Michael to Isaac. He said he had his reasons that he wasn't about to begin explaining to any Sobaski's Stairway lice.

"And you bastards know who I mean," he shouted down the steps.

Yolanda agreed to change the name, and later that

night Charlie wept and promised he would never drink again. He had been in the lockup in Frugality for ten days, and his cousin had been sent to the State Hospital for the Insane at Mayview after a vicious fist fight with Charlie. Charlie had evaded committal there himself by only an eyelash. He swore he had learned his lesson and showed Yolanda his stubby hands to prove it. His fingers were lacerated with deep, zigzagged cuts from making baskets in jail.

Charlie kept his promise for one month. He went to work for two dollars a day out of the Ford with Fats Smolcher. But one spring night he came home bloody and drunk and more frightened than ever. He continually started at sounds and did not sleep but watched the door all night. He vowed on his love for the infant Isaac that his tongue would dry up and his throat erode if he ever touched another drop. May God disfigure him, blind him, kill him if it ever happened again. He stained the baby's sheets with his tears as he stood over him blubbering.

The next day a constable came and took him to the County Jail. He had tried to run over Fats with Fats' Ford when they were out working, and Smolcher's leg was broken in two places. Fats had sent the constable and pressed the assault charges against Charlie. The reason for the assault was never clear, but Charlie said later Fats had insulted his dead mother. He didn't remember the details himself and neither did Fats. They had both stopped in the morning for a belt to get going and had been drunk all day the day it happened.

All through the smoky spring Yolanda sat at her window

waiting out Charlie's three-month stretch. She ate her black bread and tended the baby as if her husband did not exist. He did not write, but a released con on his way home to West Virginia stopped up to the apartment one hot summer day and told her he was Charlie's old bunk-buddy and that Charlie had sent the word he had learned his lesson this time. Yolanda wept and gave the con a cup of tea and a quarter. After he was gone she discovered a brass family candelabra missing; she never found out who had taken it.

In the summer Charlie came home, but he did not come any closer to Yolanda that first Saturday afternoon than the corner of Gardenia and Mechanic Avenue. Thaddeus Smolcher was waiting for him there, still on crutches; the two old friends shook hands and did not fight. They went to DeAngelo's and threw a tear that lasted all night. Fats wouldn't let his old pal Charlie pay for a single drink. And there in the back room of DeAngelo's on a hot Saturday night, elbowing swells, college boys, laborers, and whores, peace came to the two friends. While up on Gardenia Street, on the fourth floor, Ike-o whimpered and was given a cold bottle of soda pop to soothe him and Yolanda ran out of ketchup and had to get up to go downstairs to Rosie's to borrow more. *"Ets sputs,"* Yolanda said to the infant before she left, but glancing around because Charlie forbade her to speak Polish. *"Cuchi zos Bozich-kum.* Go to sleep, baby, sleep with God."

2

The sun could be shining at high noon on Mechanic Avenue, but inside, in the back room of DeAngelo's, there burned a single light bulb night and day. The bulb lit up the door to the men's room; any ladies who had need of the facilities went in the alley behind the building or took their chances on the men's room, which had once had a lock but now had a hole in the door where someone had wrenched loose lock and wood together. A favorite game in DeAngelo's was to steer visiting women into the men's room and form a line to peep.

In the back room on weekdays Charlie sat, tilted on a chair with his back to the wall, and delivered, in exchange for a round of the moon Augie DeAngelo kept in a wooden icebox, his considered opinions. He would start out from the back room early in the morning and spin around himself, like an unintentional caterpillar, a cocoon of messages, tips, intrigues, gossip, and people, until in the evening two miles away from DeAngelo's in another bar on Mechanic

Avenue some Sobaski's Stairway odyssey would have its conclusion. He would be given a tip, slip out to where Natie Phillips and the rest of the hebes shot pool by Huntz and tell him certain parties were annoyed by his intentions toward a certain Italian girl, and, with no bloodshed, Natie got the point and gave Charlie a fiver. Charlie had no friend but Fats; and Fats hung on because he knew the storm signals and could dodge Charlie when it looked like he wanted trouble by the queer way he drew in his stomach.

On Saturday nights the back room was packed, and Augie DeAngelo, toothless, eyes half closed, sat at his wooden icebox and sold Coca-Cola bottles filled with white lightning at fifty cents a bottle. He wore a coin changer like a streetcar conductor. "I got a cash register," he used to say, "somebody wants to rob me they know just where to go — with this thing they got to kill me to get my money." On slow weekdays he rented out his cot in the back for two dollars, three if he furnished the girl. A score of Charlie Hartwells, drinking and one telling a bigger lie than the last, couldn't bring in more than two dollars in an afternoon. Augie felt no compunctions about asking the boys in the back to take their business down by Rebecca Goldstein. They always came back the next day. By Rebecca there was no sleeping allowed unless a man bought his drunk there, no women but her, and no cards. And she gouged a nickel deposit on her Coke bottles filled with moon even after Prohibition was ended.

Augie was not surprised when Fats and Charlie came back to his place one September night after a political rally.

He had sent them out that afternoon when Johnny Risto wanted a fast flop and Charlie had mumbled it was the last time he was going to give up a chair for a whore; but Augie told them at the door they were always welcome, you know how business is, you don't make it today, tomorrow might be a new ward chairman. He was pleased to see them return, but, as was his custom, did not say hello to them until Fats sprung. Smolcher paid for one white Coke, and the two men went to a rear table. They sat quietly for a while, and then Charlie said, "I wish this joint had a window that didn't blow through that men's room there. Between you and the heat a man could get paralysis."

"Charlie, you ain't the man you was," Fats said.

He leaned on his elbow and fanned himself with a newspaper. His smell, of unwashed clothes and human skin soaked with perspiration, reached across the narrow table.

"I ain't in the mood for conversation," Charlie said. "And if you got to fan yourself I wish you'd go in the john, Teddy. You throw up a stink like somebody left a sewer open."

"Don't get mad now, Charlie, I didn't mean no offense, but you know how a man's mind is, it don't sit still; I was sitting here thinking how you ain't one half the Charlie Hartwell I used to know."

Charlie looked up, and said, "Stop fanning, Teddy, I got them crazy people of Gedunsky's on my mind, your smell disrupts me. You know somebody could make a fortune bottling you and selling you in wartime for poison gas."

Fats laughed heartily. "Or maybe pickle things in you," he said. "I guess you got as much alcohol in you as they use in a year up at the Mount Giliad Hospital."

"Not any more, Teddy, not any more."

They had come from a street meeting before the Greendale Post Office. O. C. Gedunsky was supposed to introduce the party's 1935 candidate for governor, but when he was through speaking the crowd would not let him depart. He talked for three hours in the hot September night. The Negroes had been wild; they cheered every word. "I ain't white, I ain't black, you hear me, I am your catfish, I am O. C. Gedunsky." The words from the man's strangely high-pitched voice lingered on Charlie's ear. "I ain't got your bunions, I ain't got your hunger, but what I got?"

"What you got?" the crowd roared back.

"I got your justice, yes. I got your justice right here, yes."

The Catfish had challenged them all with his dark eyes to prove that the two big hands he held aloft did not contain the justice he claimed. He did not lower his hands until the crowd roared its approval.

"Teddy, you don't stop the fanning I'm going to sit outside. Them raving lunatics up at the Post Office made me feel bad to begin with and you're sending over a breeze here like Mother Ida's on a Sunday morning."

Fats shook his buffalo's head sadly. "You ain't the man you was, Charlie, no offense. I remember when you and me was pals, there wasn't nothing too big for us to discuss. Now, I say one little thing and you make a grab for me."

"I am disinclined to conversation tonight, Teddy. Seeing

all those people eating up that stuff out there unsettles me. I don't know what this country is coming to."

"Have a drink. I'll pay."

"I'm off it, Teddy, I'm one hundred percent off it. I ain't a kid no more, I'm forty years old."

"Aw, Charlie, don't talk like that," Fats said. "You scare me."

"I swore off this afternoon, and I meant it."

"I swore off hundreds of times."

"Not down by Miss Fireman, Teddy, I never had nothing like that happen to me. She showed me pictures of what my insides would look like the hootch ever got hold of me. I said, 'Not for me, lady, that's scientific proof.' "

Fats leaned forward. "One little drink never hurt anybody," he said. "If you got it really licked you'll have one drink, pay your bill, and walk out like a gentleman."

Charlie shook his head. "She said if you don't take the first, you ain't liable to take the second," he said. "She's a grand woman, Teddy, it might not do you any harm to go down and have a talk with her. I notice you don't handle the stuff like you used to. You must have brought up five buckets. Damn!" Charlie laughed in reminiscence.

"It was some bad pork I ate," Fats said. "Whiskey don't bother me one way or the other."

Charlie looked around at the empty back room. "Miss Fireman said if some of the trash in Sobaski's Stairway drank less there'd probably be a damn sight fewer voters for Gedunsky too."

"Now wait a minute, Charlie, you got something personal in that," Fats said, "you know I got seven kids now."

Charlie then looked at him blandly. "You told me Marg got that way from stuff in the sheets, didn't you? Why would I want to accuse you of getting drunk and abusing your poor wife?"

His wife and daughters were one subject Fats never wanted to discuss.

Fats took his half-empty Coke bottle and poured the moonshine on Charlie's head. He marched out of the door, looking as if he were tilted backward by the tremendous thrust of his stomach. Charlie brushed the remains of the hootch from his hair and laughed.

It was a warm evening and he decided to take his small son Ike-o for a walk. The boy was four. He sat on the front steps at Gardenia Street but jumped up happily to go with Charlie. The boy was a good walker. Charlie and his son often walked into every saloon on Mechanic Avenue in one night.

In Freddie's Saloon Charlie gazed with a vast disdain at the men leaning on the bar. "Give us both a ginger ale, Freddie," he called, and said when he held the two glasses in his hand, "Yes, by God, it's Charlie Hartwell, the man with the stomach of iron, keeping it just that way. Peddle your poison elsewhere, Freddie, I got news for you — alcohol is for the backache, it ain't fit for Charlie Hartwell's intestines. I just left a drunkard — yes, he turned my good, clean stomach."

The ginger ale was cold on Ike-o's teeth. The glass was cold in his hand. He gulped the ginger ale quickly, pushing back with his tongue the ice cubes in the glass.

"Where's your best pal?" someone called to Charlie.

"Who?" Charlie asked. "Whorehouse John? That's the very drunkard who just turned my stomach."

The men on the bar laughed explosively. Ike-o pushed in closer to his father. Charlie caressed Ike-o's hair while he stood over the boy, one foot on the bar, alert, waiting for a remark to send off further sallies.

His father's fingers in his hair were warm; Ike-o leaned in closer to be stroked. He nestled against Charlie's pant leg when Charlie patted his face.

"Hey, Charlie," someone called, "I hear Gedunsky said your vote was in the bag. He said you was riding the donkey to victory in 1936."

The men in the bar laughed. "That'll be the day, won't it, Charlie?" Freddie asked. He was a tall man with horn-rimmed glasses that made him look as sagacious as an educated owl with larceny in his heart; he was brilliant only at breaking up fist fights. He would fall on the floor clutching his chest, but mostly his ability lay in spotting the trouble before it began. He observed Charlie carefully. Charlie Hartwell was one of the most notorious trouble-makers on Mechanic Avenue, a snorting bull in a pasture of suspicious red-eyed cattle. "That'll be the day," Freddie said, "when Charlie Hartwell's vote is up for grabs. Not saying there ain't plenty in what Catfish Gedunsky says, but there just ain't nobody telling my friend Charlie what to do."

Ike-o felt proud of his father. He drank his ginger ale, listening. He knew that the man talking had said something to please his father; the patting on his face had stopped while his father listened and then resumed again happily.

"You're damned tootin'," Charlie cried. "What do I look like? There ain't no wool grows on me. I'm all man."

Someone sent down a drink. Charlie downed it in one gulp, and his eyes watered, then flared. He wiped his mouth with the back of his hand. He thanked no one. If they were thinking they were going to make a fool of Charlie Hartwell, then the lice had another think coming. One drink Hartwell: no more. Good Sense Hartwell.

"Let me tell you people something," he said. "I was talking to an expert on the drinking situation just a day or two ago. This expert got statistics to prove that drinking is the sickness of the poor and ignorant. The three go hand in hand. You sell out your manhood for what's in them damned fancy bottles behind the bar. What is it keeps you poor? What is it gives the Pope his hold on you? What is it, by Jesus, that fills up the crazy house? Hootch, you lice. Whiskey." He ground his fingers together, gnashing them into mangled hooks and other grotesque shapes. He swaggered around in a small circle, holding his hands out before him. "You see," he hissed, "the two things go hand in hand, your stupidity and hootch, your dumbness and whiskey." Ike-o watched reverently; there was never such a giant among men as his father — he had quieted the whole saloon. No one spoke. Ike-o was proud that it was his daddy who could stroll so majestically, spit so angrily, talk so eloquently that he could quiet a saloon.

"I been thinking over the situation," Charlie Hartwell said, dropping his voice, "and I've been doing some reading on the subject." Charlie wiped his eyes; there was not a sound in Freddie's. "You deserve Oscar Gedunsky!" he shouted. "Study the Roman Empire! Study the fall of that noble civilization." He was invulnerable in his uncertainty; the Romans had fallen, hadn't they? "Hootch and circuses, the same thing is happening today," he cried, "the goddamned same thing."

Charlie took his son's hand and pressed it proudly. Ike-o squeezed his father's hand back just as proudly. Charlie took a deep breath. He owed them one more lesson and slowly picked up someone's drink from the bar, downed it as a Roman emperor would, nobly, without blinking.

"History repeats itself," he said bravely. "I'll personally give a ten-dollar bill to the first real American to spit in Catfish Gedunsky's eye. We fought the British and beat them and we fought Kaiser Bill and beat him too. By God, we can beat Gedunsky and his likes too." He held his shirt where his lapels would have been on a suit jacket. "History repeats itself," he said, and blinked at the apparition in the doorway and then blinked again until all the men on the bar turned to look where Charlie stared.

A real Catfish Gedunsky, the bona fide barbered and clean-shaven somber man with the hollow eyes and the brooding downturned mouth, applauded. He stood almost with no motion at the door and clapped his big, swarthy hands together.

"Have a drink, Charlie," he called in a voice hoarse from the evening's exertions. He lifted a filled glass from the bar and walked to Charlie Hartwell and handed it to him.

Charlie knocked the drink to the floor. "I drink American," he said, striding out with Ike-o by the hand.

The hoots behind them did not mean to Ike-o that his father was being ridiculed. He heard the Catfish laugh, and say, "Ah, Charlie is okay," and it did not mean to him that his father was already beneath the capacity to cause anger, that the dignity involved in being accepted seriously had been denied his father. The shouts and slaps and laughter that followed them out of Freddie's meant nothing to the boy. Ike-o held close his father's hand, sure only of the triumph there.

Up above Mechanic Avenue there lived a daylight. It twisted and swam in the air with neon wings and fins of red and green and a white all its own. At night it was there when the other, the short, false day was gone. But where Ike-o's daddy walked, there the light stayed too. The world was one long, reaching shadow into which Daddy strutted and, like the pretzeled lights above Mechanic Avenue, he drove back the creeping darkness.

"Ike-o, my boy," Charlie said as they walked home that one night, "I wish you were a little older to understand better what I'm telling you. Next year there's an election for the presidency of the United States of America and, by God, it's going to be curtains for Gedunsky and the rest of his vermin. In 1936 you're going to see such a landslide vote it will make your head swim if you were old enough to understand."

It was a long boyhood, full of things that Ike-o did not understand. In the little boy's mind it was not the light that came first but the shadows falling long and flat on the streets and sky. Only up above Mechanic Avenue was there a certain daylight, and there Ike-o watched the neon lights swim and fly. The shadows broke before Daddy. He talked and joked, laughed, coughed on his cigarette, danced a jig in the saloons, and strutted down Mechanic Avenue with no shadow bold enough to block him. He was daylight itself in the boy's imagination. The boy worshiped his father. In the dumb, dangerous world of concrete and fat, helpless Yolanda Hartwell, his daddy spoke great wisdom and crackled like a firecracker lighting up the long night of Ike-o Hartwell's boyhood.

3

Miss Sarah J. Fireman knew no holidays. The Fourth of July, 1938, she kept her office open as usual; and the benches along the walls of the abandoned poolroom and health store where she convened her office were packed with drunkards, wife beaters, car thieves, lewd daughters, and kids with diseases, as usual. They jostled each other, their heads too full of trouble to go outside and watch the fireworks display O. C. Gedunsky set off on Harris' Hill: the man who could get a job if he had safety shoes, and the lady whose piles had taken a turn for the worse. At midnight Charlie Hartwell slunk in, without shoes but wearing blue-striped stockings and with a white shirt that was ripped down the back. He ignored the two women waiting on one of the benches before him and walked, or staggered, directly into Miss Fireman's cubicle when the man to whom she had been lecturing walked out.

"You bother too much with them niggers," Charlie said, grasping to make it seem he had come to reprimand her. "I can remember when a nigger on the Fourth of July as much as took his life in his hands to walk up Mechanic Avenue, and look at it now. That Gedunsky made it so a white man got to learn how to dance to keep from being shoved off the sidewalk by them. Well, Old Charlie don't do the Charleston for nobody, I got as much to say about what goes on here as Mr. Black Sambo Gedunsky. My people was the second family here. You listening, Miss Fireman, I said they was second. Right after the Jewels come the Hartwells. I ain't about to get off the sidewalk for no one."

He tapped his pockets for cigarettes. He looked up at her quickly. "You listening to me?" he asked.

She nodded her white head. "Yes, I am, Charlie, but I've heard you tell me the same story before. I'm waiting for you to tell me why you're in this condition. A month ago you told me if I ever saw you drunk I could call May-view for you, that you would be ready to be locked up as incurable."

"Ah, I ain't drunk," he said. "I came here for you to get Yolanda to let me in my own house tonight. See, I took the kid downtown today to see something special, it being a national holiday, and the minute I showed my face back here she took the kid and locked herself and him up and I can't go home."

Miss Fireman took off her double-strength glasses and wiped away tears of fatigue from her eyes. "I can't say as I blame her, Charlie," she said, "you haven't been much of a husband."

"I might have took a drink now and then," Charlie said, "but a man has to have some little pleasure."

Miss Fireman shook her heavy white head. "I would

be the last person to deny you your little pleasure, Charlie," she said, "but you have to take your pleasure apart and look at it like it would be part of something bigger. If it hurts anyone else, it's not pleasure any more, your pleasure is part of someone else's pain."

She said it as if she had not said the same thing every night for the past fifteen years to someone who only wanted a little pleasure: a woman grown mannish with age and the burdens of the misunderstood, a heavy-faced woman who had thought she would wear a white uniform to show off a trim figure and would capture a doctor and live comfortably somewhere and raise children and had found herself instead unable, because of that moment's necessity, unable even to walk away from her desk in the poolroom, not to say Sobaski's Stairway entirely. There would be no one to listen and help if she were gone, and, recognizing that terrible necessity, she sat at that desk and grew mannish with troubles and old with no family of her own.

"I know you don't think much of what I promise," Charlie started.

"I didn't say that, Charlie, it's never too late."

"Well, this time I mean every word I say. I took that little boy of mine downtown, that boy of mine is seven years old now and he loves me like nothing you ever saw."

Later the building where the poolroom was housed would be rebuilt and would take on dimensions of its own as Miss Fireman and the old place collected things. The building would twist and curve backward and sideways with an auditorium and classrooms, a flat low-ceiling extension in the back to cover a swimming pool. Anything that came her way she would gather to her like a flower on the ocean floor, stopping weeds and flotsam. She begged from the prostitute's pimps and madams, the numbers writers, the politicians and shopkeepers slides and swings and a sandbox. And later she conducted classes in birth control and citizenship for immigrants and drew pictures on her blackboards to emphasize points that might otherwise be missed.

"There is nothing like the love of a child, Charlie," Miss Fireman said. "You will have to straighten yourself out for him, not for me or Yolanda."

"I was a kid myself, Miss Fireman, I wasn't always old Hard Luck Charlie Hartwell. I swear if them hunkies and niggers hadn't come to crowd a man and eat food supposed to have gone to him and take jobs coming to him I wouldn't have been in the sorry state you see now." He did not mention the Jewish conspiracy he fancied controlled International Banking but skipped it because the rumor was that Miss Fireman was Jewish; a person couldn't tell anything about her but that she was on the level.

"Charlie, nobody set you up as a judge," Miss Fireman said. "I've told you fifty times not to worry about things you can't do anything about."

Her eyes watered and made the little red-haired drunkard before her swim away for the moment. She blinked her eyes to recapture him and yawned. He wept softly and moaned as if to himself.

"I don't mean nothing to you," he sobbed. "Why should you care about my troubles? You ain't no kin of mine,

I'm putting you to sleep. Just get me back into my place tonight, Miss Fireman, and I swear on my dead mother you'll hear nothing but good about me. This holiday brings her into my mind, and on her memory I swear it. I ain't ever going to do anything to bring disgrace on that darling boy of mine. I been a mess, Miss Fireman, it was that no good Polack Smolcher who steered me wrong, but, by God, I'm going to be walking on Charlie Hartwell's own two feet now."

He raised his right hand high in the air to make his regeneration official. Miss Fireman sat listening and immobile. He did think, though, that if a man had to get drunk the Fourth of July was the right time, a wonderful national holiday, wasn't it? But that was all behind him. He asked her if she was listening, because she yawned again. She had him wait on the bench outside until she heard the problems of the two colored women who still waited.

At two-thirty in the morning she went with him to 432 Gardenia Street and had Yolanda admit him into their apartment. And she walked back alone, slowly and unafraid in the treacherous Sobaski's Stairway darkness, because she knew it was a well-known fact in the neighborhood that the old nurse never carried anything valuable enough to steal. She lived at that time in two rooms behind the office in the abandoned poolroom on Mechanic Avenue and had a reproduction of a Van Gogh self-portrait over her bed, the one with the bandage on his head where he had cut off his ear to give to a whore.

Charlie was drunk by ten o'clock in the morning on the

Fourth of July in Ike-o's seventh year. He would not listen to Yolanda's protests but dressed the boy in a bow tie and his white and brown shoes and put on his own head a straw skimmer; he brushed Yolanda aside when she told him that he was too drunk to take the child anywhere. "I have business, woman," he shouted, and pushed her, but Yolanda, when aroused, was as strong as he was.

She resisted and they wrestled before the front door. Ike-o ran whimpering under the bed. He lay cowering where he could not see his mother and father. "You punch me, Charlie Hartwell, I'll punch you back," she screamed at him. A missing front tooth in Charlie's wise smile had been a result of a previous fist fight with Yolanda. Charlie grappled with her, trying to push her from the door, but she would not move. They both panted with their exertions; and Ike-o began to howl like a wounded dog.

Yolanda pulled him out from under the bed and clung to him. They often cried together, each for their reasons, and that morning was no different. Yolanda wept because Charlie couldn't keep a promise. He would not keep away from the booze. Ike-o bawled with a fear that these two people would kill each other.

"You promised that good woman ninety times you was off the stuff," Yolanda sobbed, "and the first chance you get you turn on her and in the morning too."

"I didn't promise nobody nothing," Charlie said, reaching for the boy. "I said if I was so inclined I was going to stay away from the stuff a month or two until my sour stomach passed. I never promised Miss Fireman anything, you understand?"

They compromised; Charlie took from his pockets everything but enough change for a streetcar ride into town and back. He laid two crumpled dollar bills on the kitchen table and raised his right hand over the money. "I swear on my dead mother's grave that I'm going to take this boy downtown to see something special, and then I'm going to turn myself around and come back," he said solemnly.

"Wait a minute, wait a minute," Yolanda said. "Before you put your hand down, add on there that you ain't going to get mixed up with Fatty Smolcher today in no way, shape, or form."

"Him!" Charlie snorted. "He ain't no better than O. C. Gedunsky or a nigger to me on the Fourth of July. Woman, this is an American holiday. My people would turn over in their graves I gave a hunky ten minutes of my time today."

He took the boy downstairs by the hand and met Fats on the corner. Fats had a pint in his belt like a pirate carrying a gun. They swigged gaily in the street. They talked over their plans and decided Sobaski's Stairway wasn't good enough for a white man on the Fourth of July since Gedunsky had taken over. They boarded a streetcar; Charlie decided he was going to show Fats too the grave he remembered from his childhood. It somehow didn't seem right to be taking a Polack there, but Teddy wouldn't part with his bottle. He had to take him.

Charlie fell asleep on the streetcar.

It was a big day for Charlie and Mamma, because the Fourth of July fell on a Sunday and Mr. Talbott, the boss,

gave the whole office staff the following Monday off so nobody would say Uncle Sam's Birthday had cheated them of
a free day. Mr. Talbott usually spent holidays with relatives, Mamma said, and only years later, when Charlie
had learned the score from the wise guys on Mechanic
Avenue, did he realize the relatives were a wife and two
children. It was now the twentieth century, that was
something exciting to say and think about and feel, and
soon Mamma said men would be flying through the air
flapping their wings like birds. Charlie could hardly wait.

That Monday there was a matinee extravaganza at the
Alvin, and for three weeks Mamma and Charles made plans
to see it. The tickets, both orange and crisp with bold black
lettering, lay in Mamma's drawer on top; and Charles
would stand before the open drawer and gaze at them as
if already seeing the elephants and hearing the music.

On every ordinary weekend Mr. Talbott came to visit
Mamma in their little frame house on Fourteenth Street.
He stayed Saturday nights, Mamma explained to Charles,
because they had much office business that had to be done
way into the night. Unfortunately, it became too late for
him to put into his brief case the many papers spread out
on the dining rooom table before the last bus from Greendale went to town. He never made the last carriage,
and Mamma graciously let him use a special room on the
first floor she kept tidied up for guests. But there were no
other guests besides Mr. Talbott.

Some days Charles had the whole day alone with
Mamma, days like Christmas Day, Fourth of July, and
New Year's Day, and Charles loved those days and was

happy when the boss spent them with relatives. And so was Mamma, Charles could see it in the blithe, schoolgirl way she danced around on weekends when Mr. Talbott did not come. Sometimes it seemed to Charles that Mr. Talbott owned not only the brokerage firm but the little frame house on Fourteenth Street the way he strutted about on Sunday mornings in red silk pajamas and demanded the dry cereals he kept on the breakfast shelf for his health. Ordered all the way from Battle Creek, Michigan, special, he said, and nobody else was permitted to have a spoonful. He was an elderly man and his digestion was bad.

Monday was a cool day, more like March than July. The sun was not shining, but the lace curtains and the window were bright from the luminous sky outside. Mamma kissed him twice on his cheek, then held him away from her sadly.

"You remind me of your father," she said, "you look more like him every day."

His father's postcard which Charlie found among Mamma's effects had been dated Ottawa and was unsigned but for some stranger's finger marks. I Took All I Could Stand Now If I Was So Bad Get Along Without Me.

"He couldn't have treated me worse if I was a hunky," Mamma said.

"Who, Mamma?"

"Nobody, son, just nobody."

"Mamma, please don't be mad at me, I can't help it if I remind you of Daddy."

"That's not it, do you hear? That's not it."

"Please, Mamma."

"I'm not mad at you, Charles, I'm not mad at you," she wailed and put her palms to her ears. "I'm not mad at you."
Mamma washed her face again and suggested, because the day was so cool, that they walk to town along the riverbank.

He held Mamma's hand tightly and listened to the rustle of her clothing. Her perfume colored the morning air with an extra delight for Charles. She was an attractive woman, slender and erect, soon to die, but that luminous morning her paleness, even the unnaturally rigid posture that concealed her pain, seemed right to the boy. Everything about the fifth of July seemed right: the heavy but bright clouds overhead, the river flat and gray but not blinding to the eye, and a coal tugboat churning along as they walked and watched it. The paddle wheel on the boat was as comical as the bobbing white tail of a funny duck swimming downstream.

"This was all part of your family's farm," Mamma said. "Your people have been here since 1794."

"Why don't we chase the hunkies away?" Charles asked. He did not like the bearded strangers.

"In some ways we're no better than they are. The way the Hartwells treat us we could pass for hunkies. I wish your daddy had lived, we wouldn't be on bad times, Charles. Not for one minute."

Charles wished Daddy had found gold in Canada. He also wished he could meet those Hartwells who were his cousins and the richest people in Pennsylvania and whom he was not allowed to talk about unless Mamma mentioned them first.

"Daddy's part of the family had a little hard luck in the depression of 1874, and Daddy's relatives did everything but shove our side," Mamma said. "But I'm as respectable as they are, I'm just as respectable. It ain't easy raising a boy without his father helping out."

"If Daddy found gold them other Hartwells would tip their hats to us."

"They'd be the first in line," Mamma said vehemently.

At First Street, the last street on leaving Greendale and the first coming in from downtown, there was a bathhouse operated by a man named Feeney. There was usually a crowd of men who sat on milk boxes before the place and played checkers, spit tobacco, and talked politics. Feeney was the ward chairman, the first Irishman so honored in Greendale, which had been of a predominantly Dutch, German, and English stock. The men playing checkers or cards seldom looked up.

Mamma took Charles' hand to lead him across the railroad tracks away from the men at the bathhouse.

"Yoo hoo, blondie," a man called. Others chanted, "Blondie, what are you selling?" and meowed like cats after her as she quickened their pace.

"Pay them no mind," Mamma said. "Remember you're a Hartwell. Your people had footmen when their ancestors were tending sheep in Ireland."

Greendale was like a stew where every element combined with every other element and nothing was ever secret. Mamma was a prime topic of conversation before Feeney's bathhouse; and Charles knew that the sudden silences when he walked within the sound of the men's voices meant that there was something involving him being said. Not until he went to stand before Feeney's himself did he know the sort of conversations that had been halted on his passage.

Mamma walked quietly and thoughtfully the rest of the trip into town. Once she called the men before Feeney's "lice" and then said no more about the catcalls that had followed her. She stopped before the theater, and looked down at Charles.

"It's fitting that today is kind of a holiday even though it's not the Fourth," she said. "I'm going to show you today who them hoodlums was defaming, son. I'm going to show you today before it's too late."

He could not resist. "Give me a hint, Mamma, please."

"Not one more question."

The audience was gay; they laughed at everything on the stage. They made sounds of wonder at the great show. There was a chorus of girls dressed in Arabian harem costumes and they sang out songs appropriate to each part of the world the funny man visited, and the girls were all as beautiful as Lotta Faust or Mae Phillips; and two giants came out and wrestled and climbed on each other's shoulders and walked off the stage on their hands. Mamma squeezed Charles' hand in appreciation of the magnificent extravaganza on the stage; and there was an English pony ballet at which the audience stood up and applauded the amazing gyrations of the smart little animals. And finally came the moment when the great stage was flooded with light and the grand finale march began and the audience drew in their breaths as a seemingly endless line of elephants paraded across the stage and huge nigger slaves marched along beside the beasts and the beautiful Arabian girls scattered rose petals where they walked. The audience stood when it was all over, and Charlie with them, and he shouted with the rest, "Bravo, bravo, more, more," but anyone knew such entertainment could never be duplicated. Charles' heart pounded as if he had been running a mile.

Mamma's face was flushed when they came out of the theater. The day had turned more gray than bright, and people hurried with their heads down in the wind to catch trolleys for their homes. Mamma took him by the hand again, after buttoning his collar tightly and securing his scarf, because the wind was cold. They walked quickly through the streets. Charles was excited but sleepy; Mamma was in a no-nonsense mood, she pulled him along as if he were a rag doll.

She all but shoved the hurrying people aside when one blocked her.

"There," she said when they came to the steps of an old stone building. The building was of a moldering stone, and it leaned like a sick man resting against the wind. The grass before the place was high and mostly long weeds that swayed with the late July wind. Mamma held Charles' hand firmly as they climbed up the crumbling steps. "This is the First Presbyterian Church, it has to make way for the twentieth century," Mamma said, but had to stop because she was gasping for breath.

"Charles, this is the twentieth century," she continued. She talked slowly, afraid to lose her breath again. "This is nineteen hundred and five, and you saw down there at the Alvin that it's the greatest time in the history of the world to be alive. When else, Charles, could ordinary people like them in the theater be privileged to see such sights like live elephants and such singing? Never before, Charles, that's when — never before, but it's an everyday happening right now in America. Long as you have the money there ain't one pleasure a person couldn't have in nineteen hundred and five. But time doesn't stop for any man or any man's feelings or any woman's either, and what we want ain't always what time gives us."

She looked at him sadly and he knew it was because he was only a boy and not supposed to understand anything. Mamma held back her tears; because it was her duty, and the boy was fatherless, she had to continue even if her seriousness fell on the gray wind.

"This beautiful old church now is going to be torn down," she said, "and it ain't all because it's ready to fall down. There's a bunch of real estate people wants to put up a livery stable, and this church is on valuable property. I would have never brought you here, Charles, but I read in the paper where they're going to raze this right down to the ground. And in a way this is your property as much as any real estate man's even though you ain't going to get a penny from it. But things have got to move, and if it's a livery stable they want, like Mr. Talbott says, it'll take the devil to see they get otherwise."

Charles nodded soberly as each idea came to him. He did not like to hear about Mr. Talbott's sayings now. He wanted the day to be private of the strutting figure in red silk pajamas.

"Mr. Talbott says there ain't another country in the history of the world where any boy had as much right to think about being President of the United States as Mr. McKinley or Mr. Roosevelt did," she said. "This is a great country, do you understand, Charles? This is a great country, no matter how many Greendale hunkies spit tobacco juice on it."

She paused for breath, but it did not come. She coughed and leaned on the iron railing of the steps.

Charles feared she would pitch back down; she seemed to have no control of the spasms and thrust a handkerchief into her mouth as if to choke off the hacking cough. Charles stood dumbly watching her. She inhaled several times and took him by the hand, not looking at him, and as Charles remembered it later Death walked with them too but unnoticed, already a sure part of Mamma because there was an utter silence about her and a yellowness like that of a decayed leaf.

"I must tell you this one thing," Mamma said.

She tapped with her black-gloved hand a small, rotting tombstone. The weeds around this grave were as high as the stone.

"We have something nobody in the world can buy, Charles, and there ain't nobody privileged to sell it either."

The tombstone read:

Colonel Isaac Hartwell 1737–1807

Brandywine, Trenton, and Princeton
A Great Patriot and Soldier
Sorely Lamented by the United States.

"There's a real man under that ground," Mamma said, "and he's as much your ancestor as he is the ancestor of all the other Hartwells running around Pennsylvania with their noses in the air. There's something you got under this ground there ain't fifty Feeneys can steal, although I'd bet a cookie they'd try. You got honor, Charles, honor, say it over to yourself like it had honey on it. You got that man's blood running in your veins; and when you're a man and you have things to settle in your brain it'll be part that great hero's brain working for you." She stood as proudly as if the stock had not watered down to Tommy Hartwell, too afraid to say good-by to a woman, a watered-down bravery and imagination culminating in this dull, thick-headed little boy.

The boy watched her, sensing that this was the important moment. "No Irish need apply," he said.

Mr. Orrin Talbott sold the frame house on Fourteenth Street a week after Mamma died four years later. She had not been well enough to work in the brokerage office that last winter, and Mr. Talbott had absented himself for longer intervals. They could not be sure which weekend he would come and leave Mamma her twenty-dollar bill; they knew privation. She fried pancakes every night for supper, and she did not seem to care when she died in her advanced state of tuberculosis. She closed her eyes and sighed as if something good and not death was about to happen to her. Charles took a room on Short Street near the Universal Car Company, where he emptied out spittoons and swept the splintered wooden floors. He quit high school at fourteen. In the evenings he stood before Feeney's

Bathhouse and talked dirty with the other men until there was no one left, and then he went back to his room and stared at the wallpaper and cried because he missed Mamma.

Charlie, Ike-o, and Fats meandered down a long alley downtown. Charlie and Fats took turns carrying Ike-o who was sleeping; but even in sleep he clutched and did not drop the pink Kewpie doll Charlie had won for him at a firing range. They blew in all of Fats' money working a coin-motivated lift for flashlights and fountain pens and throwing balls at a pyramid of rubber milk bottles. They won the doll firing at clay pigeons, but Fats couldn't win anything and protested to the manager of the joint that his gun barrel was crooked, and they were shown the door. They were staggering too badly to fight, and Ike-o began to cry.

Charlie shook his fist at the men inside the penny arcade but picked up Ike-o and hobbled after Fats. They had given up looking for the place where Colonel Isaac Hartwell's bones lay: there was no livery stable at all downtown. Then a hustler propositioned Fats, and, not having a dime but horny on the spot, he followed her. And Charlie and the boy followed him down a long dark alley near the Monongehela River.

Fats went into a rooming house after the woman; and Charlie stretched out on the sidewalk to close his eyes for a minute. When he woke up his shoes and straw skimmer were gone and someone had stolen the boy's Kewpie doll too. It was dark, and Charlie stood and scratched at himself. A urine circle had spread at his crotch where he had relieved himself in his sleep. His head hurt; he rubbed it, walking along in the night under a street light trying to figure what had happened to Fats. He decided after a while to go home.

The lights in town were lit and people strolled along down Fifth Avenue and along Liberty Avenue, and some turned to look back at the man without shoes and the little boy. Ike-o held his father's hand and skipped along with him. He thought, in that moment of summer in a city of warm night and lights with women made up in huge straw hats and men dressed in white flannels, that he had the best father in the world to take him to see such things.

Charlie walked along barefooted, damned be the starers and pointers; his young son clutched his hand and the two of them were a team that could resist an army of dudes and madams. "Hey, you!" Charlie cried. "See this boy, he got royal blood — what can you say for yourself, Marmaduke?"

The man who was being denounced smiled, took his lady by the elbow, and walked around the wild man and the boy.

"Hey, Marmaduke!" Ike-o piped. "What do you have to say for yourself." But the man did not turn, only walked away with his white-silk-suited shoulders broad and level. "Tell him, son," Charlie said, "let them hear from you."

They walked further down broad Liberty Avenue. They seemed to Ike-o to be the only ones moving while the street and the finely dressed people halted and waited for them to speak, to cry out, to press a button and turn them on. The air was soft and warm and waiting too.

"Say, Chauncey!" Charlie shouted across the street. "How would you like a bust in the beezer, right above that mussy?"

Ike-o nodded happily when Charlie told him confidentially, "Cowards, pack of lice — they wouldn't dare make a fist at me."

It was good to walk with this lord of the summer night, this hero and warrior: Ike-o skipped along, filled with pride that no one in the world would answer his daddy's challenges. He was the king of Liberty Avenue, the still, summer night, and life too.

"Oh, oh, Isaac," Charlie said, "there's just the man I'm looking for."

He left the boy to stand against a plate-window store front and sauntered after the priest.

"Excuse me, father," he said, "but it's one of our own in a little bit of trouble. I need two dimes to ride my son and myself back to Sobaski's Stairway."

The priest was a young man but hard. He demanded to see the son. Charlie led him back to Ike-o.

"Is this your father?"

Ike-o nodded his head, and the priest gave Charlie two dimes, but the mean fellow walked with them to the car stop and saw them aboard the streetcar for Greendale. Ike-o did not sleep on the trolley; it was the greatest day he had ever known. "There, there," Charlie said proudly when the boy kissed him.

They were joyous walking down Mechanic Avenue; O. C.

Gedunsky was setting off his fireworks from Harris' Hill, and the glare illuminated the street and the faces of the crowd. They were all made the dazzling color of the flares and rockets.

Mechanic Avenue was their home and the fireworks were for them. "See that," Charlie said, holding the boy on his shoulders. Up there in the air it was only a few feet higher, but Ike-o felt closer to the explosions in the sky. He felt himself to be spinning, a whirling flare himself in his insides. From up in the air on his daddy's shoulder he could look down Mechanic Avenue and see all the good, happy lights of home while up above the personal fireworks crackled just for Daddy and his boy.

"Oh, look!" Ike-o exclaimed with the crowd, blending his voice with the "ohs" and "ahs."

"The American flag," Charlie said soberly, "and goddamn Catfish Gedunsky for a hypocrite."

There was seriousness now: the profundity of adult causes and ideals. There was an importance even to being Charlie Hartwell's son and watching fireworks. The glare of Gedunsky's fireworks from Harris' Hill illuminated the street and the faces of the crowd. Before their apartment Yolanda stood. Her face was mottled the pale yellows and greens of Gedunsky's display.

"Mamma," Ike-o gasped, "you don't know what we did today."

She snatched the boy from Charlie's arms and ran with him into the apartment house.

"Mamma, nobody would fight us and Fats got lost and we won a Kewpie doll and we lost it and a priest gave us two dimes." The boy would not sleep; he held her hands trying to tell her of the wonderful day, the day like no other, the Nation's Birthday and a day of warmth and stillness and excitement and Daddy's victories over all the things that would try and shove him around.

"Come, baby," she finally said. She held him, wearing only white training pants, at their window, where the colors of the fireworks splashed their faces and the sides of the buildings. "Mamma," he said, sobbing with desperation and fatigue, "I just can't tell you about the Fourth of July. I can't tell you about today — there was too much."

"I know plenty," Yolanda said, her great round face impassive by the rockets overhead.

Charlie saw his wife at the fourth-floor window with Ike-o and did not think that anything was amiss. He watched the fireworks himself and even talked to the new Negro tenants of 432 Gardenia Street. It was when, dog-tired, he went upstairs to sleep for the night that he realized he was locked out. He hammered on the door and threatened to break it in. He went in his blue-striped stockings and ripped white shirt to Miss Sarah J. Fireman to see if she would intercede for him with Yolanda. Gedunsky's rockets burst mockingly over his head, but Charlie Hartwell was too tired to shake his fist at them.

4

Metro Sobaski, the man not the legend, slipped on his own wooden steps one night. The steps were not icy but falling to pieces in many places; after his monumental job in building the stairway up high Harris' Hill, Sobaski had done nothing further. The steps were on his property, and he did not repair them and had one of his ankle-top shoes caught between two slats and went crashing down to Fifteenth Street. He landed on his neck as had so many other people.

His daughter, whom he had sent away to a New England college, did not come home for the funeral in October of 1940. She had married, and, because no one had ever met her husband, it was believed in Sobaski's Stairway that he did not know the source of her father's wealth.

Although Metro Pius Stanislaus Sobaski had no relatives, the funeral was well attended, hate mingling in the smell of lilacs and disturbing the tranquil air around the shaven corpse. One man, a local drunkard named Torachek, spit

into the face of the dead man as many people had told
Sobaski they were going to do. The mourners felt a glow
at the moonshiner's death and the indignity upon the corpse
itself. They felt they had outlived more than a mortal but
their hungers and an abstract fear, as if he, the flaxen corpse
with his face clean and powdered and his miner's hands
clasped in a peaceful gesture never seen in his life, had
actually been the shame and poverty they had lately en-
dured.

Charlie and Fats went to the burying ground with a
Jewish tailor and drunkard named Seigel. They fought
over a bottle of moon that Seigel had concealed inside his
shirt, and, in a rage, Seigel threw the bottle against a rock
and broke it. The news of Hitler and concentration camps
in Germany had excited Charlie and Fats. They often discussed who would go and who would not if they were the
dictators of Sobaski's Stairway; the afternoon of Metro
Sobaski's burial they screamed at Seigel that he was one of
the first Jews marked to go.

They left the tailor and joined a group of Negroes who
were passing around a bottle of Four Roses. They borrowed
eighty-five cents from the men after riding back to Sobaski's
Stairway with them. They summoned Ike-o to them and
explained to him a plot they had contrived.

"I'll go out front of Augie DeAngelo's," Charlie said,
"and start rolling around on the pavement. That won't get
Augie stirred up, he'd let me die out there, but I'll moan,
'Bloody murder, Augie's moon killed me!' "

"And I'll lift you into his back window, Ike-o," Fats said.
"You know where Augie keeps the moon in the icebox?

Get your hands on what jugs you can and fling them through the window. I'll catch them jugs, don't you worry, kiddie. Old Teddy will be there right under the window to scoop them up. There won't be a drop spilled."

Charlie and Fats could not control their laughter; they poked each other with volcanic glee. Ike-o was a tall boy but slim and obviously slippery for his nine years. He did not join in their jubilant dance on Mechanic Avenue. His face was overcast with grayness and his chin trembled.

"What's the matter with you?" Charlie asked.

"It's stealing," Ike-o said.

"Ah, kiddie," Fats said, "it ain't stealing when it's Augie DeAngelo's moon. Me and your daddy paid him sixteen times over for the stuff. It's legally ours."

"What's the matter with you?" Charlie demanded. His throat was dry from the long day, and his patience was short, as narrow as the distance between him and the trembling boy. Charlie held back his good right arm, which normally would have landed immediately in a swift back of hand on the boy's cowardly cheek.

"People are put in jails for stealing," Ike-o explained. By their happy conduct Ike-o was not sure that Fats and his father understood. "You get put like an animal in the zoo." He ventured to make it even clearer. "The teacher said it ain't right to take something don't belong to you. She said Melvin Thretakis should be ashamed. He took some girl's comb."

"Why, you cowardly little son of a bitch," Charlie said, letting his just right arm do further expression for him. He knocked the boy to the ground and stood indignantly by

while Fats soothed the kid and helped him to his feet.
"There, there," Fats said, unnecessarily.

Ike-o did not cry. He trembled and his face was very
gray. He looked down at the ground, apparently thinking
something of his own.

"It ain't stealing," Fats said, "when it got the okay from
two respectable older people. Mind your father and me,
kiddie, we know what we're doing."

Ike-o did as he was told. He slipped through the back
window while Charlie moaned on the sidewalk and assembled a small crowd. Ike-o tossed through the window four
pints to an eager Fats in the alley; he climbed after them
hastily, landing on the cobblestones outside on his side.
His elbow hurt.

"Sure thing, old buddy," Fats said, not complaining when
Charlie gave the boy their accumulated eighty-five cents
and another quarter to boot for work well done. Fats decided Ike-o was a queer kid — for all of his beefing he
snatched the money eagerly and shoved it into his pocket.
"Ah, that's more like it," Fats said, and poked Charlie to
indicate his appreciation for the happy greed and normalcy
of the boy. But Fats was sorry for Charlie Hartwell that
his boy had shown himself a coward like that right out in
broad Sobaski's Stairway daylight. Fats and Charlie both
kissed Ike-o for bringing them the hootch in such fine
fashion. They sauntered up Mechanic Avenue with the four
jars bulging at their middles. They sang.

Under a street light, Fats and Charlie killed the first pint.
Then they wandered up Second and Third Streets, where
the Jewish tenements were, and sang. "When Hitler comes

to Pittsburgh, we'll be there," they caroled, "oh, we'll be there." Their melody was from "When the Roll Is Called Up Yonder." The Jews watched them somberly from their windows; Charlie and Fats took bows, blowing kisses to the silent people. The moon and their mood, the tense faces and the death of Metro Sobaski safely under their belts, they were ecstatic.

"Here," Ike-o said when they were out of sight, giving Augie DeAngelo the dollar and ten cents in change, not looking at it or Augie but putting the pile into DeAngelo's hand.

"I'll chop your hands off next time you put them in my property, kid," Augie said.

He rang up the change in his streetcar conductor's register. "It ain't adequate pay for four pints of moon," he said, "high-grade stuff, get a deuce a pint for it." He glared at Ike-o, who decided to wait no further for a reward. Ike-o had been told in school that honesty would be rewarded somehow, somewhere. He sighed and said, "Thanks, cheapie." He felt good inside anyhow.

"Cut your fingers off one by one," DeAngelo said. "Keep them in your pockets, I got a meat cleaver under the counter for thieves. I get a deuce a pint for that stuff."

The next morning Ike-o found his father on the doorstep at 432 Gardenia Street. He was in a coma from alcohol, and someone had drawn on his face with a burnt-out match the Star of David. It looked like dirt at first, but, standing back, Ike-o saw it was the six-pointed star of the Jews. Ike-o never told Charlie what had been done to him.

Fats was found the same morning by the police. He

was soaking in the watering troughs for horses before the Mechanic Avenue Station. "I went to sleep," Fats explained, "and when I woke some criminal had filled the tub up with water."

"Big fellow like you," Charlie said. "I'd have put up some struggle before anybody dunked me like that."

"I'd like to know the clown's name who tried to drown me," Fats shouted. "I been to a squire and he said there are plenty of laws to protect a citizen against felonious drowning."

"It's funny a big guy like you don't like to fight," Charlie said, stepping out of reach. "Why, my boy Ike-o can take better care of himself than you can."

Fats was not called by his nickname because of his size, although he was as large and unwieldy as a water animal, but because his nickname vaguely rhymed with his given name, Thaddeus. He was also known as "Whorehouse John," but never within his hearing or for any one reason; the name might have come from his frequent visits to Mother Ida's on Fourteenth Street or from the fact he lived in a house with two insignificant sons and six women, including the youngest, Dolly, and his wife, Margaret, all of whom had reputations for promiscuity.

Margaret, the mother, entertained local young men in the family porch swing behind the house. A generation gossiped about her and bragged they had left their cherry with her, but it was mostly small boys' talk. Margaret selected only men who were passing through and liable to take her with them on any train leaving Sobaski's Stairway for any place better, which, to her mind, was anywhere else. She loathed Fats and slept with him only when there was no one else to entertain in the porch swing.

Bertha, Rita, Dorothey, and Irene grew up in a Sobaski's Stairway where men straggled through the streets at night looking for women. They were all seduced at early ages and did not rebel, but sometimes did it 'for money or sometimes for a proof of a true love affair. They were attractive girls when they were young and had many true love affairs, most of them culminating with Fats threatening to "Kill that son of a bitch, he shows his face around here again." There were innumerable fights before the Smolcher home on Sixth Street, long nights of slow cars circling the block and honking the girls remorselessly. Fats could shake his fist at the cars, but he could not outrun them. And, too, a disappointed suitor was liable to empty a garbage can in Fat's front hall or throw a brick through his window. Fats resigned himself to suffering in silence and visiting Mother Ida's on Saturday nights. He went without his old friend Charlie. Charlie, being American, did not seem to Fats to have the same sex instincts he did; he never went, but had many excuses. Fats thought Charlie Hartwell the purest, most intelligent man he had ever met. He often spoke of "Charlie and me" even when Charlie had no connection with the story. He believed but for some bad breaks, which Charlie had suggested but never outlined, Charlie Hartwell could have been President of the United States or at least an alderman. He had said so himself. Fats was as pleased as a father could be when Ike-o, the kid, came calling on his youngest daughter Dolly.

When Charlie caught on, he ran all the way from Four-teenth Street and Mechanic Avenue to Sixth Street. He banged on Fats' door with both small fists. He was cold sober.

Fats did not open the door quickly. He never did, especially with Charlie. "Them men who read a lot," he used to explain, "you never know what's on their minds." Charlie had often been seen reading detective stories.

"Charlie, you come friendly, okay," Fats called. "But you come looking for trouble, you better forget it. I don't want no trouble. I'll call a police, honest to God."

"Is that so?" Charlie hissed. "I think it'll be me calling a policeman, Mr. Whorehouse John, you don't release my son."

Fats was distraught at the indecorous name, but he did not become angry.

"Your son ain't here. You hear me, your boy ain't here."

"Now, I'm warning you, Fats, that boy is fourteen, I don't want him associating with any of your daughters."

Fats became enraged. He picked up a shovel he kept near the door for protection. He threw open his front door.

"Charlie," he cried, "you say one dirty word about my family I'll bring this down on your head."

The sight of the shovel calmed Charlie. "I came here friendly," he said. "There's no reason for you to get into a huff. Put down your shovel. I came over here friendly to tell you Ike-o is too young to be thinking man's thoughts. You know I don't have no bad thoughts about any of the fine girls in your family."

"You better not," Fats said, "considering the kind of name

your mother had here in Greendale and Yolanda too. There was plenty talked about her until I put my foot down. I wouldn't hear it."

Charlie choked.

"You mentioned my mother," he gagged. "You went too far that time, Mr. Whorehouse John, there ain't anybody doesn't know what goes on in your house and on that back porch swing."

"Ouu," Fats moaned.

"You're raising a pack of whores, everybody in Sobaski's Stairway knows it. You hear me."

Charlie shouted now for the benefit of the curious people bent out of windows watching and listening.

"A pack of whores," he called. "They ought to all be locked up. Don't talk to me about a policeman. It's me who's going to be swearing out charges for a raid. I don't want my son to be mixed up with any of your daughters."

Fats ran into the house.

"He's going to get a gun," someone shouted down from one of the windows.

"Let him kill me," Charlie shouted, spreading his feet apart. His impression was that Fats was running upstairs to throw a bucket of water down on him as he had done after several doorstep arguments; he hoped that Fats still did not own a gun. Charlie stepped back into the middle of the street. "Charlie Hartwell doesn't run from man or superman," he cried.

Fats walked out into the middle of the street, holding by the hand a little blonde girl. He walked directly up to

Charlie. He was crying and with his free hand brushing at his face. He could not control the contortions of his huge features; his nose twisted with his mouth in one direction, then another.

"Here," he blubbered, "here's the child you called by that name."

The little girl looked from one to the other of the men. She was thin with high bones in her face and a small serious mouth. Her eyes were a pale blue but deep. She was thirteen, but seemed younger because of her pallor and the childishly inquisitive manner in which she looked from her father to the other man.

"This is my daughter Dolly," Fats said, "you been maligning out here for these Jews and niggers."

Charlie blinked his eyes once more. "Honest, Teddy, I didn't even know you had such a daughter. She's even more a baby than my Isaac. When I heard up at Poole's my kid was seen with one of your daughters I thought right away it was Bertha or Dorothey or maybe Irene. Now I know you're their father and all, but you got to admit you wouldn't want one of your sons to be running around with them."

Fats fell to his knees on the cobblestoned street clutching the little girl. "Daddy, please," she said.

"This is my baby," Fats said. "There ain't none of them counts but this one. There ain't never going to be anybody going to say one lousy word about this baby."

"You're damned right," Charlie said. "She looks like a fine girl."

"The rest are too," Fats said, still clutching the little

blonde girl. "People just don't understand, them girls got too much life in them." A smile creased his huge face. "Them girls ought to be in Hollywood."

Charlie smiled too at the happy thought. "You're damned right," he said. "They're better looking than most."

"Hollywood," Fats whispered happily.

The little girl stole back into the house, leaving the two men. They argued whether they would go to a state store and buy a fifth or drink away their combined five dollars shot by shot at Freddie's.

5

Ike-o and Dolly walked the back streets of Sobaski's Stairway, finding security in the blank dark faces sitting on stoops and at second-floor windows. They did not expose themselves to the neon lights of Mechanic Avenue. They avoided the clerks in the pawnshops who leaned on trunks, the barbers who peered up from cutting hair to comment on the street, the humbugs congregated around mailboxes and waiting for the day's number to be announced at four o'clock. They followed a daily route of alleys and narrow streets from Our Way to Chauncy Drive to Riverspoon Street, then down along the warehouses at Pasture Way and out to Fifteenth Street by way of Short Street, along the deserted loading platforms of the bankrupt Universal Railroad Car Company.

They did not know most of the people on their route. Negroes had infiltrated Sobaski's Stairway, house by house, street by street; the Polish, Syrians, Jews, and Italians were fleeing as if the new immigrants constituted the army of a hostile country. There were many street fights between the old settlers and the new arrivals; there was a race riot at Greendale High School. In Freddie's the men said it was inevitable, but despite frequent rumors and predictions, there was only that one outburst and no more.

Because it was dangerous for a girl alone in the back streets of Sobaski's Stairway, Ike-o and Dolly met in public places, before the plate-glass windows of Top Dollar Sammy's, Bosco the Processor, Professor Chandu's Health Store, and the Golden Star Sanitary Supermarket; they were seen before these Mechanic Avenue places meeting, and this was how the older Hartwell learned that his son was courting a Polack and a daughter of Fats Smolcher.

Charlie tried tact. He told Ike-o that the Hartwells were a distinguished American family, that he was too good for a daughter of a drunkard and wife beater like Thaddeus Smolcher.

"I'm part Polish too," Ike-o said.

"Son, the Polish strain in you is about as strong as the whiskey in a mixed drink by DeAngelo. I think the rest of what you are makes that part almost invisible — you were raised American, that makes a difference. The Hartwells were the second family here."

"I'm one-half Polack," Ike-o said, "there isn't anything you can say can change it."

He had known Dolly for a long time; Ike-o thought now that his feeling for her was love. He had arrived at this conclusion after much thought. He did not make decisions quickly. Sometimes he could not make up his mind at all. He was impatient with himself. He usually became violent and fought often. He would put his head down and charge wildly, but the resolution he expected never came from a contact of his fists on flesh. He was left stymied; he did not like to fight.

He believed he understood no one in the world except Dolly. "You're my girl," he told her many times, liking the idea that he was not alone or peculiar because he was some strange breed of coward.

Ike-o and Dolly decided they were different. "Don't laugh," he told her. "Ain't it good for us we found each other?"

Ike-o's thoughts went around in circles; they sometimes left him exhausted. He brooded a great deal, not knowing even where to begin thinking about some things, like his family or sex or Sobaski's Stairway.

He caught on to his schoolwork easily. But for the sake of the dopes and hard guys in his classes he pretended to be slow; he swore loudly in the school corridors, thinking he impressed some of the classier girls from Mount Giliad who went to Greendale High School too. He was very strong, but he was not interested in sports; he thought all sports to be fixed. He watched most things jealously, through gray eyes speckled with red dots and envy for people better poised than he was, better dressed, or better looking. His big fists flailing away at an enemy were not enough; somewhere the questions came, ringing in his ear and calling him loser even while he heard flesh pounded and saw blood, "What am I doing? Oh, God, what am I doing?"

His features were regular except for his forehead, which was heavy, and his chin, which was small. He was powerfully built, and of the things he brooded about he knew a great deal about sex; but not with Dolly. He promised her that their first time would be on clean white sheets some-where at least a hundred miles away from Sobaski's Stair-way. She was fourteen then and it seemed to her that that was exactly what she wanted.

They had known each other from the first grade in Miller Public School onward. He did not remember a time when he was not enchanted with her blonde hair and deep, hurt eyes.

"If I was to die," she asked him, her pale blue eyes not leaving his own, "what would you do?"

Ike-o thought over the dreadful possibility. They sat on the wooden steps of Sobaski's Stairway, looking down on the black, tar rooftops below. Occasionally they stood to allow someone to pass up or down.

Ike-o touched her cheek gently. "You ain't about to die," he said. "Why ask something like that?"

He held her face in his hands. "I'll never marry anyone else," he said, "I promise."

"Don't promise a lie."

"I swear it," Ike-o said.

The long Sobaski's Stairway night sat down below on the gray streets like an impatient guest. The night cast quick, long shadows on the rooftops. Ike-o and Dolly were a long time in the ache of youth and desire and separation.

One of Dolly's sister's true sweethearts had recently tried to trick Dolly into going down to Wheeling, West Virginia, with him on the pretext that they would watch the trotter races. She had flatly refused, telling Ike-o of every gesture, the words he used, the promises.

"It's the only thing a woman got," Ike-o said. "She gives that up she's only half the person she was."

"How about to a man she loves?"

Ike-o brooded on the question, turning it over into the crannies of his own experience and the engraved stone rhetoric of Mechanic Avenue conversation. There were no books in the Greendale Public Library on the subject, no books anyhow for Ike-o Hartwell and Dolly Smolcher from Sobaski's Stairway, where the love act was done mostly, when there wasn't a lookout necessary, in all the accumulated privacy a curtain could give. "It ain't right until the two people are married," he said, relying at the last moment on the bad things that could result and canceling out heat and desire. Marriage was an ultimate perfection. And big, shameful bellies, disease, hoots, and the protective arm of Goldstien the Pimp, Mr. Henry, and Little Ned the Duke waited for girls dumb enough to come across for love. Ike-o had, however, never observed one right marriage. He imagined that with his own stunning union there would be an answer to all of the confusion in his world. "There ain't no percentage in doing it before marriage," Ike-o said, bluffing. He was ashamed to say before Dolly that he regarded the love act as sacred.

But he worked both sides of the street, walking with the tender, nervous fingers of adolescence entwined in the pale hands of his Dolly, and up on Pig Alley and Eighth Street doing another twist. At fourteen he cut a wide path. Only a man as preoccupied with weighty problems as Charlie Hartwell was would have believed that Ike-o had not a direct and involved relationship with the faded flowers that bloomed behind the stout oak doors off Mechanic Avenue.

Ike-o had been taunted from ten years on for being a virgin. He was called "Cherry" and "Sister" by older boys, and, at twelve, too shy to admit that the white girls at Mother Ida's had turned him down for being too young, had started to visit the colored joints, especially Miss Mildred Brown's. Ostensibly he went there at first to sit sprawled in the torn chair in the waiting room and listen to the music from the jukebox.

He had finally been accepted at thirteen as a paying customer, cash first, as befitted a man who was liable to refuse to pay and tear up a whorehouse if he was not satisfied with the action. He saved seventy-five cents every week for the purpose. He liked the ceremony more than the act upstairs on the beds with street mud at their feet and no blankets or pillows because they were not intended for sleep. He liked the places, the admission by everyone around them that the world was blue and rough and loud and mostly ugly, and listened to it in the saxophones, clarinets, trumpets, and bass fiddles and drums that spoke on the jukeboxes with the voices of the girls upstairs on the dirty beds. He talked knowingly of the oefay. He held the Yardbird in his mind as a personal possession. Whose song said it better? He discussed with the girls what great talents blew gage and shot themselves full of horse just as even the most degraded upstairs. At fifteen he was given five dollars a week by Miss Mildred Brown for steering high school classmates to her place. He was thought by everyone, except his father, to be a very hep and wise kid.

Sprawling there, foot dangling in time to the magic music, he treasured Dolly. The blue world of raids and garbage cans and disease was made only a parcel of a bigger thing. Happiness waited him. Dolly was his dedicated mission; they would arrive one day at a heaven on earth.

"I ain't got a mother, I ain't got a father," he said, dropping down beside her on the grass behind Greendale High School. "If I don't have you I don't have anything."

"It's you who's special," she said, pulling his head close, whispering into his ear. "It's you, you're like a big, strong horse tied up, pulling, pulling."

He was a big, strong horse with her. He was The Man, Clark Gable and Billy Conn and strong, fast, smart, and a comer. He could close his eyes, leaning his head on her bosom, and the world was all her fingers on his face and his importance. There was no ugliness and no little red-headed man who strutted like the king of Ethiopia while a fat woman followed him around worshiping him. He pressed closer to Dolly.

Only at night did they kiss, once or twice at the front door of her place on Sixth Street. "Hold me close like that, honey," she used to say. "Oh, Ike-o, just like that." The night was almost in their hands; they almost owned it. "Not now, Dolly, there'll be plenty of time later." She held him, not moving, breathing against his cheek. "I love you, Ike-o." The arrival of goodness and light was postponed. It was subdued and swallowed in his throat. "Not now," he said, "we have forever." There was no death or confusion or night. He would kiss her perhaps twice, knowing that on Sixth Street at Fats Smolcher's door there was not time for more.

The Smolcher girls had active reputations. There would be a sister coming in or going out or someone patrolling the sidewalk or the street with his parking lights on. It was better that they waited for the clean sheets in the future. They agreed, before Ike-o was sixteen, that they would marry when he graduated from high school.

"What's going on?" Charlie asked him, after Ike-o had been seeing Dolly regularly for three years.

"I'm going to marry Dolly Smolcher," Ike-o said. By his small smile it was difficult to tell whether he ribbed.

"Over my dead body," Charlie said.

"I want you to live forever, Dad," Ike-o said, "don't say things like that."

"You don't show me the respect due a dog."

Ike-o picked up his schoolbooks and went out to the Greendale Public Library. He liked history; he studied it more than the other school subjects. It gave him a feeling that life was bigger and broader and deeper than Sobaski's Stairway. Men lived and died and would continue to live and die, and the aches and confusion were only in his own chest. He spent many afternoons in the library reading history books indiscriminately, dreaming over them of adventures not his. When he was not reading in the afternoon he was shooting pool at Spook Novakovitch's cellar poolroom. He met Dolly every day he could.

She was remote in his mind from the act over at Miss Mildred Brown's or Mother Ida's. Ike-o and Dolly feasted on the feeling. It could have lit up every house in Sobaski's

Stairway, Ike-o thought, sitting on the steps and watching the houses below become rectangles of lighted windows. He sat alone on the steps some evenings, remembering Dolly. She now had lovely, long white legs and red lips and soft, blonde hair, but to him this was accidental to his feeling. She was his pure Dolly, innocent and unreal even when Ike-o was with her.

He kept her name out of street-corner conversations. He knew the reputations of her sisters and her mother. Her brothers stood on corners and at bars, lounged against pawnshop trunks and the posts of street lights, and waited. Like Fats, Ray and Steve Smolcher were in a perpetual fight that erupted in many small sorties in poolrooms, bars, and street corners to clear the family name. Steve asked him directly.

Ike-o shook his head violently no. "Does it make sense?" he asked. "I intend to marry her." Steve had heard that one before. "You better see that you do," he said. He carried a blackjack he threatened to use on anybody messin' around his sisters. He was twenty-five years old and had acquired syphilis somewhere. He wore a patch on his nose that he changed every day.

The night of Ike-o's graduation there was not a black or dark blue coat to be found the length of Gardenia Street. Charlie had gone to find one that afternoon, but he had not come back, and the commencement exercises were due to begin in half an hour. One of the requirements of graduation from Greendale High School was that every scholar wear a black or a dark blue suit coat or sports jacket. The rule kept no less than ten boys a year from attending commencement. Their diplomas were mailed them. Yolanda ironed a light summer dress slowly. She hoped Charlie would allow her to go to the commencement. She lingered over the ironing board, wishing not to disturb Charlie by dressing up and making him think a decision had been made without him.

"Okay, okay," Ike-o said, "they'll mail me the diploma. Do they have to hand me the thing for it to be legal?"

His mother paused in her ironing. The dress was almost hot enough to burn. Yolanda waited with her eyes at the door for Charlie. "Maybe Papa got hit by a machine," she said.

"Or a pint of whiskey," Ike-o said.

"It's not nice to talk like that," she said. "Papa tries for you. Look, you're going to be the first one in my family to graduate high school. Even Papa did not graduate."

Ike-o sat on the edge of the bed.

"I'm going to see the Catfish," Ike-o finally said. "He'll get me a black coat."

Yolanda turned as if the words themselves would bring a wrathful Charlie Hartwell to the door. "Don't mention that name," she said. "After the last trouble you was in with that man, Daddy said he was going to kill us all he finds you doing business with Mr. Gedunsky. You want to go to jail again?"

"I wasn't in jail," Ike-o said. "Do I have to draw you a picture to tell you I wasn't in jail?"

Ike-o had taken to stooging for O. C. Gedunsky. He could find some measure of understanding from the politician. When O. C. would put his arm around Ike-o's shoulder and promise him big things, it was better than no proposition at all. Everyone suspected Gedunsky's part in Ike-o's trouble, but Ike-o had said nothing. The Catfish owed him a favor.

"How many times do I have to tell you Gedunsky had nothing to do with it," Ike-o said. "The poor guy gets blamed for everything that happens in Sobaski's Stairway. I saw her back there, I saw the line-up of guys waiting, and I thought maybe it was a fight or something interesting. Okay, it didn't turn out so good for me because I happened to be too dumb to run from cops and the woman was nuts. The whole thing didn't have one nickel's worth to do with the Catfish."

O. C. Gedunsky, through his emissary Percy Leech, had stationed him at the head of the line. Percy Leech had told Ike-o the woman was an old friend of O. C.'s down on her luck and that the Catfish had cleared the spot back of Markowitz's with the city police.

"Is there any danger?" he had innocently asked O. C. Gedunsky.

O. C., don't tread on me, let me be, the Great Catfish, you're my dish, Gedunsky, ask your daddy, he'll spell it for you, had looked at him and Percy Leech with a hurt expression twisting up his prize-fighter's face. "Would I ask you to do anything dangerous, Ike-o?" he asked back. "You're like my own son to me."

"That's right," Percy Leech, the occasional barber, said. He was a small man who agreed with everyone he met on days he was not disagreeing. He had no in-between.

Ike-o had stood solid in the corridor leading to the court-yard behind Markowitz's. It was not the kind of place that somebody would have thought of first for excitement and romance, not like magazine pictures of a woman leaning backward on a porch swing by moonlight and maybe a guy standing somewhere outside of the picture figuring how he was going to get at the woman in the swing without both of them breaking their necks, not like that, but dark and crummy with fallen pieces of cement and stinks of cabbage, fish, and dog urine. It wasn't any more than a clearing of gray cement seven feet by seven feet bounded by garbage cans behind the delicatessen.

Ike-o had not seen the woman. Neither had anyone else in the line, but the men knew she was there, seemed to smell her outgiving sex above the garbage scent, and passed the word along down Mechanic Avenue that the price was right: any coin will get a man or boy into the courtyard past the big seventeen-year-old kid guarding the entrance. Percy Leech swore the length of the line that the woman was twenty-three and looked like a movie star. If the men balked or said they were busted, Ike-o leaned on the opposite wall and blocked their passage.

There was little argument, because any coin would do, a quarter, a half dollar, even a dime; there were mostly first-time kids in the line or horny old unargumentative bums who needed the woman bad to pass up a double shot for her. In an hour of action Ike-o's mental tally estimated more than forty dollars in his pocket. He jangled the money happily and thought it might not be the worst idea to take the woman after everyone was gone and do something himself with her. But for free, the way Ike-o Hartwell got things, not in a line-up with kids and old bums. She was a down-and-out friend of O. C.'s trying to make enough to buy some dancing costumes; hers, Percy Leech had explained carefully, had burned in an automobile accident that she was lucky to walk away from with her life. She was a celebrity, a well-known tap artist and contortionist from Wheeling, West Virginia, Percy Leech had said, but nobody could prove it by the courtyard shadows — and what was the difference? Ike-o thought. Nobody in the line had come to see her dance. Ike-o chanted his good news and thought it was great of Percy and the Catfish to set him up like this in a full partner-ship with them and the lady.

"A well-known contortionist from Wheeling, West Virginia," he chanted softly in the manner of the pimps before Miss Mildred Brown's or Mother Ida's on Eighth Avenue, "she's played before royalty in Los Angeles and Coving-ton, by God, in the great Commonwealth of Kentucky." But one of the men in line blocked the corridor. Ike-o saw the punch before he felt it in his stomach and knew the muscle was from a cop or a crook; the man did not let him fall, perhaps to crawl away to freedom, but held him up close against himself as Ike-o sagged and moaned with pain.

They had clean shaves and haircuts and their hands were uncallused for all their strength. Ike-o felt their hands in his pockets searching for weapons and taking away his money and knew from the clean shaves and smell of talcum that they were police. "Take everything," Ike-o said, "every-thing." He tried to wriggle free but they held him by the collar and the belt; he was soon alone with them in the corridor, the line-up had vanished as quickly as if the men had crawled into the decaying brickwork of the two buildings that flanked the passageway.

"Just when I got to the head of the line," Ike-o said, catching his breath. "I've been waiting here forty-five minutes for my turn."

"Every word you say is gospel truth," one of the policemen said, "it's my crooked ear, it hears things queer."

"Please," Ike-o whispered. "Please let me go, this'll break my mother's heart."

"I'll bet you give her plenty to be proud of," the other cop said. "I'll bet she wishes you were an orphan." He was a heavy man but handsome with dark intense eyes.

"I'm legit, I swear it," Ike-o said. "I was just waiting my turn."

"She legit?"

The lady's hair was frowzy by the street light on Mechanic Avenue. Her hair rested like a fish net all over her head, and she stood leaning uncertainly against a pole with her sad, bewildered old eyes blinking and her stockings down around her ankles.

"That legit?" the handsome policeman asked again.

The uniformed policeman with her was trying to cover her with his own coat. "I ain't tired," she pleaded earnestly, and pushed away the cop's coat. "I been with the whole seventh battalion once down at Fort Dix before that general or somebody like that got mad at me — I ain't tired, honest, Sammy. Try me."

"That legit?"

Ike-o batted his eyes. "She's goofy," he said unbelievingly. "She ain't got her senses."

"You neither," the uniformed cop said. "You're missing something upstairs to play a game like you was doing."

"She was represented as a dancer from Wheeling, West Virginia, to me," Ike-o said, still not able to conceive of the woman's trembling, her terror, as having anything to do with him. "A dancer," he choked out, "I thought she was a dancer from Wheeling."

"A dancer from Western Psychiatric," the handsome cop snorted. His dark eyes followed every move of Ike-o's. "The judge up in Juvenile Court is going to tell you that you was as good as tampering with a dead woman."

"I don't remember who tipped me off," Ike-o had told the detectives in the black wagon. "I just come on the thing and decided to make a good thing of it."

The handsome cop had held his big soft fist under Ike-o's nose. Ike-o watched it as light from outside flickered on it. Mechanic Avenue neon lit it, then lost it as the patrol wagon jogged over the cobbles and streetcar tracks. Because of fear and contempt for his own stupidity, that anyone would put him on to something good, Ike-o lashed out and was sorry; he smashed his fists against the beefy chests of the detectives. They punched him hard and threw him to the floor and sat on him.

"We let Percy go, but O. C. left you on a desert island this time, buddy," the handsome cop said. "There's some people downtown, not too friendly to him, want to hear his part in the deal. There ain't nobody concerned about you or Percy Leech in particular. We're going to let you off downtown if you're a nice boy and make a connection for us between the Catfish and that squirrel."

"I don't know the party you mentioned," Ike-o said, spitting.

"Let him up, Dan, " the other cop said. "He ain't got no more sense than that squirrel."

"He got plenty of sense for conspiracies."

"This kid ain't got no more sense than that squirrel — look at him, he's shaking like a leaf."

The friendly cop put a five dollar bill in Ike-o's shirt pocket when they arrived downtown, motioning Ike-o not to respond by talking. The cop shook his head sadly and made a ooo ooo sign over his head and pointed at Ike-o's head. "You got something missing, kid," he said. Ike-o made a growling sound in his throat and glared at the detective. "Fink!" Ike-o said.

Because of his age he was sent to the Thorn Hill Reformatory in Warrendale for two weeks, not sentenced but detained to have his attitudes observed and analyzed. He did not fight or argue with the cabin instructors; he had been warned by the judge that he would be released only if his conduct was perfect at Thorn Hill.

His second Sunday there O. C. Gedunsky visited, looking cool in a white-on-white shirt, barbered, every one of his grizzled hairs smooth down to his wild, white eyebrows.

Ike-o led the Catfish to the big barn where the suckling pigs were. His intention was to stab him to death with a pitchfork, but he relented when he saw his familiar broken nose and heard again the high soft voice. "I did not mean you any harm," the Catfish said. "I wish it were me here and not you. It was an old street game we played in Sobaski's Stairway since I was a boy." Ike-o wept instead, leaning against O. C.'s strong shoulder and putting his head down on the patterned white-on-white sport shirt; the Catfish had been his only visitor.

His lack of family had been listed against him on his blotter; the county kept him an additional two weeks above his two weeks of observation because of the apparent neglect. He had gone to his hearing alone, Charlie Hartwell publicly washing his hands of the affair in the back room of DeAngelo's, and Yolanda anxious to attend but frightened off by the thought of a murderous fight with Charlie and the shame of being observed by unfriendly policemen.

"Get Miss Fireman," Ike-o finally cried. "Get Miss Sarah J. Fireman from down in Sobaski's Stairway. She knows me, she'll testify to my good name. Get her — there's one person knows I ain't a criminal." He stood in the waiting room in the small executive's cottage where inmates were not permitted and shouted at a man who sat behind a desk.

"Don't sit judgment on me," Ike-o said, "until you talk to that woman. She knows my mother, she knows my father. She understands us — I ain't a criminal. You got to lock up everybody in Sobaski's Stairway you lock me up."

He was given extra toilet-cleaning details and not permitted to talk to anyone; but a week later Miss Fireman came for him.

Ike-o was released in her probationary care. She drove him home from Thorn Hill in a station wagon with the words "Jewish Welfare Association" on the side door. She tried to talk to him on the ride home to Sobaski's Stairway, but, when he sat morose and unanswering, she said nothing further. He slammed the door to the station wagon hard and went first not home to Gardenia Street but to look for Dolly. "Don't think I owe you a goddamned thing," he said to Miss Fireman before he left. "I'm not my old man to take favors from anybody, get me, I'm myself. The next time you see me, start off by saying, 'Good-by.'"

But she had that hold on him that was as relentless as the arm of a Fifteenth Street strong man, a head buster that squeezed and hurt and asked not "Give!" or "Torture?" as did the boys in the courtyard of Miller School, but, more like sighing, whispered, "See, this is the way it is, this is the way your mind and heart should turn." He tried to avoid her goodness; he looked at her, thinking he saw across the desk what she was, a woman never with a man, no kids of her own, a woman broad with big talk and never on the sick green end of charity. Sure she could talk. Talk was cheap, ask Catfish Gedunsky.

"She says I ain't a greenhorn, Catfish," Ike-o told the politician. "There ain't nothing I need from you or Sobaski's Stairway that I should trade myself away like I was a sack of potatoes or something. Catfish, I want to do the right thing, you understand?"

O. C. had shaken his head as if in amazement. He believed in what he was doing; he believed that anyone who disagreed with him was a potential thief, being already a proven liar or fool. He could lie himself, it was part of a master plan of service to Sobaski's Stairway. Talk was cheap. It could make men dizzier than whiskey, and crazier. He had never been farther away from Miss Fireman than twenty blocks, and yet he first expressed amazement that the little old lady was still alive. "A queer duck," he said, questioning her longevity as if it were as serious as repeated indictments for forgery.

"I wonder about that lady," he said, accumulating doubts as serious as old age. "Why is she not at all familiar with her language and people? I ask you what kind of conduct is that from a respectable Jewish old maid not to *parlez vous* mamma language, Yiddish, and not to grace any of our synagogues or churches here with her presence." He stopped only for a moment at her linguistic misdemeanor. "I know she has rich friends," he said, "but she could give us a break at least one holiday a year. You get what I mean about the caliber of hypocrite you've got me dealing with here?" Their quarrel was about the price of trouble. Miss Fireman handled it free, asking only that it be not repeated in the same way again, but worked with tuberculosis and cancer too, comforting when she could not cure. The Catfish wanted the voter safely in his vest pocket; that was his price for handling trouble. Nobody but Miss Fireman would have thought a vote was worth arguing. She did not vote herself; she was a registered Democrat, but she said that Woodrow Wilson himself would have voted Republican if he ever saw the Catfish out in front of thirty different polling places in Sobaski's Stairway handing out cheap cigars.

"What's your claim to fame?" Ike-o asked the Catfish. "I don't see you busting down the doors to no synagogues. Who are you to criticize anyone?"

"Take a good look, son," the Catfish said, "thank God for

me and the Democratic Party. The times needed someone
dumb and loud and could speak Armenian, and Polish,
and lousy English, and here I am. I think Sobaski's Stairway ought to put up a statue for me just for the people
I put to work for the county, not saying nothing about the
city and the state, just a statue of me for my county pay-
rollers." And bartering language for action was quick and
cheap, and then action for any kind of belief when pressed
into a corner, that was Catfish Gedunsky. Never once a rule,
not even don't spit into a friend's face on Tuesdays. Nothing. But talk, then action. And finally nothing after all.

Ike-o had not been sure of what Miss Fireman's crime was;
but that was O. C.'s trick, you couldn't get the exact meaning in black and white from his nastying. A person never
knew how to take him. He could conduct a dialogue on a
street corner with another person or deliver orations before
five hundred and no one was ever sure exactly where he
slandered or how he had evaded entrapment.

"Who me?" he would ask. "When did I ever say our
esteemed friend was unworthy? — Why, talking low about
that fellow would be like talking low about Earl Browder
himself — I couldn't say anything about the one without
bringing up the other, the kind of friends they were. What?
I don't have proof? Well, I ain't got his Commie Party card
number if that's what you mean, but I seen him waving
many a red flag right up on Mechanic Avenue. Just ask
him how he spent May Day, 1936, 1937, and 1938, and
1939 too if I ain't mistaken. Or you could ask his mother,
sure she's local, you'll find her in a crib down at Mildred
Brown's — it'll cost you two bucks, but I hear she's worth

every penny. No. I'm kibitzing on his old lady, I mean, that's a colored joint and I never seen her down there. There was no question of paternity in your mind, was there, because of the shade of his skin? No, sir, I don't take *that* route. It's her boy under suspicion — you'd think he wouldn't want to run for ward chairman all the money Moscow sends him the first of the month. And, by the way, Mr. Hartwell, where does your friend get her money?"

Yet there Miss Fireman's goodness was: more important now than Gedunsky's nastying and the humiliation of another rat named Ike-o Hartwell from Sobaski's Stairway. She was braver than any of them, as tall as the tallest, able to walk among the slum people's wretchedness and not flinch self-consciously or talk from the side of her mouth or have her eyes dart to some suspicious corner of themselves and not her. She was as good as the poorest, as strong as the richest. She spoke directly to him because she wanted nothing for herself. Her percentage was in heaven. Or somewhere better — who needed angels? Ike-o Hartwell asked himself.

"Okay," he finally said in desperation, "I'll give every chump I meet an even break. I'll smarten them up so they can sit on me, not me on them," and left Miss Fireman's office, not amused at her friendly smile and pat on his back.

"Like hell I will," he snarled, going up Mechanic Avenue to Novakovitch's Pool Hall.

Yet, he thought, wouldn't it be nice if there were no chumps and nobody around who needed to use them.

"I don't care yes or no Gedunsky," Yolanda said, "I just

tell you what Papa said. We got some pride, sonny boy, we don't take from them kind of people." She took her dress which she had been ironing for the commencement and put it on a hanger on the door but facing away from the front door where Charlie might see it.

"Aw, cut it out, Ma, we take from whoever is handing it out," Ike-o said. "I'm going to get a coat from O. C."

"I had a friend once, a Jewish lady, Mrs. Plotkin," Yolanda said, "she used to live on the first floor till her husband died and she moved by a son. Papa threw her down all the steps once. She never come to see me again. Papa don't like nobody don't act American. He means it, Isaac, he'll shoot us you fool with Mr. Gedunsky."

"Papa don't scare me, he's always punching somebody three feet tall or threatening to shoot somebody. Well, I ain't afraid. As soon as I find a job I'm going to marry Dolly, Papa or no Papa. He can shoot me, but that's what I'm going to do."

Charlie Hartwell strode into the room. His face was red from running. He gasped to catch his breath. "Is that so?" he wheezed. He staggered, carrying a black coat, to the one chair in the room and slumped into it. "Is that so, boss?" he asked. "Is it the son who gives the orders around here? I told you once and I'll tell you again: there ain't no son of mine going to marry a hunky. Your grandmother and grandfather would turn over in their graves."

"Give me the coat," Ike-o pleaded. "We'll discuss it another time. The damned thing already started up at the high school."

"We will discuss this matter now."

"Pa, the coat."

"Damn the coat."

Charlie ripped at the coat. He tore off a sleeve. He caught it by its back vent and ripped it straight up the back. "Damn the coat!" he cried. "My son is going to marry a hunky, and you got the gall to talk to me about a coat. I got this coat in a restaurant. I stole it, yes, goddamn it, your father becomes a thief to satisfy your pride, and what thanks do I get? You stand there telling me you're going to disgrace your ancestors."

Ike-o looked down at the shredded coat. "I don't understand you, Pa," he said. "I guess I never will. Look what you done to that coat. And for what? — Because I want to do the same thing you did. You married Ma, what's the difference?"

"Plenty. I knew her people. Mike Stanachek was the best man in Greendale. He was quality."

"But Fats is your best friend, you pal with him."

"I know that stinking whore chaser, that scum, I know that whole family. Don't tell me about the Smolcher girls. You'd have to hire a detective and somebody to watch the detective."

Ike-o sat on the edge of the bed. "Ma, what makes him like that?"

"I'll kill her she says another goddamned word."

"She ain't said the first one yet."

Charlie stood quietly. "I know you ain't got the respect for me an ordinary man has for his dog," Charlie said, "but I got things I can do too. You marry that tramp, and, honest, Isaac, you ain't going to find that fat lady there alive the next morning. I swear it on my mother. Now, you know I mean it."

Ike-o went immediately and borrowed a coat from the Catfish. It was an old coat, taken off on the spot by Percy Leech, and was small, but it was adequate for the night. O. C. gave him a twenty-dollar bill for a graduation gift, and when Ike-o got there the intermission had started. He mounted the platform and sat with the other scholars.

"Here it is, Ma," he said afterward, handing her the diploma.

She had come in and sat in an empty chair near the back, hardly daring to glance up to the proceedings on the stage, as if her son or the stage lights dazzled her eyes. She wept but only partly through joy; her cheek was beginning to swell where Charlie had struck her, threatening worse if she went to the graduation ceremonies, but she had gone nevertheless and wept with pain and joy.

"Fine piece of paper, ain't it?" she asked.

"It's very important," Ike-o said. "A fellow can't get anywhere without being a high school graduate these days."

But he saw the swelling and understood the tears, and outside the auditorium on the dark side steps of the school building they sat down together. There had been no group around them, no congratulations, only the twenty-dollar bill from the Catfish, the dark coat of Percy Leech's, and themselves in the June night, a tall fair boy and a fat weeping woman. They sat in the stillness outside and watched the people leave, listening to the people call to each other, but not unhappily, as if they were somehow included too in the good wishes that abounded everywhere but on the steps where they sat.

"Well," Ike-o said, "I got to see Dolly — she's waiting for me."

A breeze carried a hint of rain on it; he wanted to see Dolly and to watch her face when he handed her the diploma.

"If you marry that girl I'm a goner," Yolanda said.

"It doesn't have to be that way. Leave him."

"But that's the way it is."

"He ain't going to kill you," Ike-o said, "don't be foolish."

"He got ways of cutting a person to pieces without a knife."

"Walk out."

"Don't say that," she said, "there'd be nobody to take care of him. What would people think of me, huh, if I left my husband?"

They sat in silence, feeling the soft wet touch of the night wind. They could hear it rustling through grass and sifting dust on the steps. Over on their left the lights were turned out in the auditorium and the night became momentarily darker and then light again with gray-white racing clouds over a moon in a hurry.

"What do you want me to do?" Ike-o asked. "I planned to marry Dolly soon — do I got to think of something else? There's plenty of work around. This ain't no depression time. This is 1950. I planned to marry soon."

"What about the army?"

"I'm not due for six months. A person could live a good

lifetime in six months. I want to marry Dolly bad, Ma — she's for me. We got something good."

Yolanda sighed. "I ain't got no right to ask anything of you," she said. "I never done nothing for you."

He took her little fat hand quickly and pressed it to his lips. It was hard with calluses but he held it close to his cheek as if it were soft and comfortable. "There ain't nothing I wouldn't do for you, Ma," he said. "You raised me as best you could. You taught me what was right as best you could."

"I was always religious," Yolanda said. "There ain't nothing like a good upbringing."

"What shall I do?"

"Don't marry that girl yet — let Daddy cool down. He's awful mad."

"Goddamn him," Ike-o said. "Damn his soul."

"Don't say that," she said, "it ain't right."

He walked with her home to Gardenia Street and then trotted down to the Smolchers on Sixth Street. He took from behind a garbage can a glass pickle jar with small stones in it. He walked past the Smolchers' house quickly, rattling the stones in the jar, then jumped over the fence into the Smolcher yard and stood under the back window.

There was no light, but his heart pounded when he heard a window open. A stranger would have heard only the night breeze scattering newspapers down Sixth Street.

"Ike-o!"

"Dolly, come out, I have to talk to you."

"I can't, I can't, he's been prowling around all night with a shovel. He's after someone. You can't stay."

"My mother, she wants I should enlist in the army right away."

"What about us?"

"I have to talk to you," he whispered. "I got to explain. You have to understand."

"What about us?"

"It'll have to wait," he said and knew she had closed the window. "Dolly!" he whispered. "Dolly!" But there was no sound except the lonesome wind.

Ike-o placed the glass jar on her doorstep to let her know he meant business. There would be no further need for signals between them if she intended to be unreasonable. He looked away quickly fom the Smolcher house. Thad Smolcher was known to drop things from his window down on people who loitered uninvited at his front door. The rain on the wind had not arrived. Ike-o walked down Mechanic Avenue slowly, beating time on his leg with his diploma; he wanted to buy someone a beer, but he found no friends in any of the saloons. The moon came out, but it was not as bright as the neon or the street lights. Ike-o took his diploma, and, balancing it on his index finger, he made his way down to Gardenia Street.

6

Ike-o had begged all of them to stay away; only the Catfish was to come with him to the railroad station in Greendale, but the politician had a meeting and Charlie insisted
on accompanying Ike-o. He could not refuse Yolanda
either. She dressed herself in her cavernous yellow commencement dress that was too light for the cool June evening. She had not washed her neck; Ike-o saw the dirt
there and hoped the other boys from his graduation class
who had enlisted would be too busy with their own parents
to notice his. He could not reach Dolly. The Smolchers had
no telephone. In desperation he had sent her a telegram telling her he was leaving for the army that evening. He had
not seen her in four days. She was in none of their usual
meeting places; he had walked from one to the other
searching for her.

"You look like a yellow hippopotamus three sheets to the
wind," Charlie told Yolanda. "Why don't you stay home?
This is man's business."

She wept in her silent way, not quivering for all her weight, but motionlessly, focusing her eyes on him in disbelief. She knew that he could bring it to pass that she would not go to the station. She believed Ike-o was going to be killed in the train ride up to Maryland. She wanted to see her only child this one last time. She wept silently, watching Charlie, trying to gauge how deeply he felt. If he wanted her to stay he had his tricks for making it happen his way.

"You look fine," Ike-o said. "I couldn't leave unless you come down there with me."

The railroad yards stretched from Sobaski's Stairway at First Street almost to downtown. Ike-o asked his father if he would be good enough to call a cab, but Charlie had other plans. He wanted to walk the ten blocks to the railroad station.

"The hell we will," Ike-o said. "You ain't going to parade us into all them saloons again tonight. I know you, Dad, don't do anything like that tonight."

Anybody who walked up a street in Sobaski's Stairway with Charlie Hartwell had to promenade from bar to bar where he had this old friend to see or that guy who promised him a fiver on a job. Ike-o had spent years outside of every saloon in Sobaski's Stairway waiting for him to untangle his complicated business inside. He usually made Yolanda wait outside too. He never had enough to buy her drinks and did not wish her companionship.

"Not tonight," Ike-o said, "just not tonight."

"If you tell me you're leaving a neighborhood where you was born and raised without saying good-by to Augie

DeAngelo or Freddie or Mrs. Rebecca Goldstein, then you're no son of mine. You're a monster, that's what you are. How can you walk away from them people known you since you was a kid?"

Charlie was steamed; it appeared to him that the boy's going away was not going to result in the acclaim due a long-sacrificing father and maybe the riotous free, yes, free because of the patriotic nature of the occasion, drinking up and down Mechanic. He saw that Isaac understood his motives and that made him angrier. "Go to hell then," he said, and tore off his necktie. He sat on the edge of the bed glowering at the floor. "Go to hell and take that hippo in the yellow dress with you," he said. "I assure you, my fine son, she ain't welcome here after tonight. You just let her show her face around here after all the conniving you and her done against me the last eighteen years. Goddamn, you two made my life a hell."

They walked as Charlie wanted them to down Mechanic Avenue, stopping in DeAngelo's, Freddie's, and Rebecca Goldstein's, where they found a snoring Fats Smolcher. He was unconscious, half in and partially on the floor of a back booth. His head lay in a puddle of beer. Charlie shook his head disapprovingly and said to ignore the damned lush.

Ike-o shook hands with Mrs. Goldstein as he had done with the other saloon owners while Charlie graciously put away another drink. "I want you to remember, Isaac," Charlie said loudly, "that you're going to meet all kinds of people in the United States Army. I don't want you to hold a man's color or religion against him. A man is what he is inside, not what God put on the outside. Jew, Negra, Catholic, I say a man's a man. We all worship the same God, only in different ways. Right, Rebecca?"

The Negroes at the bar shuffled away; it was impossible to tell which way the wind might blow his emotions the next minute. Everyone avoided him; Ike-o reminded him that Mother waited outside and that the train left Eastern Standard Time, not Daylight Saving Time. Charlie left grandly, shaking hands. "I say a man can't hold it any better than Fats ought to leave it alone," he whispered going out. "Look at what a family I saved you from. Them people have got a taint in their blood."

Yolanda stood patiently outside like a docile sheep dog guarding the crowd of humbugs and tramps congregated on the sidewalk. Ike-o was furious but determined for his mother's sake not to say one word. There she stood, pushed forward by a drunk and then lumbering aside to make way for two drunks who swaggered down Mechanic Avenue, their arms about each other's shoulders.

Her face had been molded by fat and quiet into folds of Buddha-like repose; there was nothing that happened on the street that could penetrate into the good, soft recesses where she lived. She got as much out of the world, Ike-o thought, as a lamb. If she were to lie down on the sidewalk, her head in the spittle and her toes in the garbage on the curb, would one person walk around her, one person say, "That's a human being, pal, don't walk on that"?

"I'd cut my throat for you, Ma," Ike-o said, taking her arm. "Don't worry about anything."

She waved her hand at him silently; she did not want to start Charlie again.

Ike-o would go to five armies for his mother. She was a brave woman. She had hid him in her skirts from his father and gone to stand in lines for free food from the Catholics, the Salvation Army, the Jews, anybody who was handing it out: answering a world of questions to be allowed to dine on the sick, green food of charity. Walking ten miles additional she had marched around Sobaski's Stairway to save a dime on a quarter pound of butter and bought with it ten penny Tootsie Rolls which she hid in her bosom and brought out at night to eat five and give the beloved infant Isaac five. Going to the army was the only way he knew to protect her; he would have to settle with his old man someday, but there had never seemed to be a worse time. He thought he had made the wisest decision. He did not know what to do about Dolly; he would write her. She would understand. If there was nothing else sure, there was this one thing he had: Dolly and Ike-o talked the same language.

Ike-o's anger cooled by the time they came to the station. His father carried his suitcase proudly, waving to strangers and winking at everyone he saw.

Yolanda wore a fixed smile; she realized the depth of her love every time she looked at the boy. He was of her own people, a Stanachek, the build, the speckled gray eyes, the straight way he stood. He could have been all of them, Michael dead at twenty-eight, Stan at thirty, Doris at sixteen, Mark, smiling little Johnny still a baby but dead in Purgatory, Frieda, Ray, Helen, Alex. She cried soundlessly for all of them. Ike-o put his arm around her shoulder and his mouth close to her ear.

"Don't worry about anything, Ma," he said, "I'll be okay."

"You're all I got, baby, don't let anything happen to you. Ma will cry every night till you come home."

He held her close, unashamed of the dirt, of her unsightliness in the grotesque yellow dress. "Take care of yourself, Ma," he said, "just take care of yourself."

Charlie started to shake his hand man-to-man.

"Things are going to be different when you get back, Isaac, that's a promise."

"I understand, Dad, I understand."

"Maybe I wasn't a saint, but when you get to my age you'll see things ain't always what they look like."

Porters and the crowd moving toward the platform pushed them apart. Ike-o gripped his small suitcase and walked with the crowd. He did not look back to see them.

"Don't take any wooden nickels." He heard Charlie's voice.

Ike-o bent his head, feeling tears coming to his eyes. He passed through the barred gates to the train. After eighteen years, he thought, there ought to be somebody, somebody a person would want to see when they leave their home. After eighteen years you'd think there would be one person anyhow who felt like saying good-by to a guy on his way to service.

He turned first to the boy walking with him when the boy spoke, not to where the boy pointed. "That blonde chick's waving at you, man," the boy said.

She was standing in front of the black oily wheels of a

train. Her pale eyes were sparkling, whether with tears of sorrow or happiness he could not tell; and when she saw that he saw her she partially raised her bare arm but did not complete the gesture. She held her arm over her head, suddenly uncertain that he would approve of her singling him out by calling, "Ike-o, Ike-o, it's me." Her dress billowed out around her as people brushed past her. A porter bumped her and continued walking quickly down the concrete platform. She could have been a statue but for the billowing lavender dress.

Ike-o dropped his suitcase and walked toward her. Not even after he kissed her did she drop her arm. When she did, she rested her small white fist in his hair. "I love you, Dolly," he said, barely audible. "Thank God, you came."

"You knew I'd come," she said, "you must have known." They held each other. "I'll wait," she said.

"Promise," he said.

"I promise," she said.

He sat alone in the back of the train. It was not dark outside yet and he could see the rooftops of Greendale when the train moved toward town. The neon lights danced in the window glass.

The single bulb above DeAngelo's back door looked like a beacon of home against the huddled, dark Mechanic Avenue. Ike-o wished he were going toward it instead of away. Where was his home, that a bulb above the back door of a saloon could make him soft and fill him with a music bigger than all of Sobaski's Stairway? He let the feeling pass, remembering the split Polish skulls and the tired old whores, legs punctured by hypodermic needles into elephant scales, who sat in the back room, and the spilled generations of vomit staining DeAngelo's woodwork.

There had been a rumor in the newspapers that Sobaski's Stairway, all one hundred and ninety-five acres, was going to be torn down by a Pennsylvania state redevelopment commission. Ike-o watched the passing street lights, the gray buildings muffled in color by the late light until they looked like stored-away furniture with sheets on them. There had been rumors that Sobaski's Stairway was going to be torn down since he was a boy. The tenements had been condemned for years, but there was not enough room yet in the federal housing developments for the people of Greendale; they lived on in the leaky, drafty old buildings. He saw a bum vomiting before Freddie's. He saw the bum wipe his mouth with his sleeve and stagger in the growing darkness back down Mechanic Avenue. Ike-o thought that the rumor was not true. He listened for a while to some of the boys on the train singing their school fight songs. Downtown they picked up more recent graduates bound for Maryland. Ike-o settled back to write Dolly a letter. He hoped Thad Smolcher would not steam it open but did not give a damn if he did. He intended with all his heart, he thought, to marry Dolly as soon as his three years were up, if not sooner.

Dolly thought that Ike-o worried excessively about her. She thought that she loved him and would be forever faithful as she had promised him. She did not think it would be hard to avoid men; she had one-half semester more of high school before she graduated, and there was no one in the classes of Greendale High School who attracted her. There was hardly anyone who knew her. She walked to and from school quickly, without any friends.

When she was not with Ike-o she had daydreamed about when they would be married: shy girl dreams that went up to the bridal bed and no further. She wrote him that she loved only him and could not wait for his first furlough or pass. She drew a circle around the part of her letters where she had kissed the paper. At nights, alone in the room she shared with her sisters Rita and Dorothey, she imagined him holding the paper to his lips and kissing it in the exact spot.

In her loneliness, after two months of sitting on the edge of her bed in the dark, flowered bedroom, hiding as much as participating in the life around her by studying movie magazines, she made a move. Or rather, she did nothing when Dick Eastland, a football player from Mount Giliad, asked her to go with him to a school dance; and when she did not say no but went to the dance and met him there, not expecting him to come to her house, and danced with him and felt herself envied, she said nothing when he talked of that coming Saturday night. But at eight o'clock she stood on the corner near Linoleum Way, the short street that ended in a small bridge between Mount Giliad and Sobaski's Stairway. Getting into his convertible, accepting a cigarette, she did not know why she was there, observed herself, and knew she cared nothing for Eastland. "I love Ike-o Hartwell," she told herself emphatically, and that somehow made it easier to sit with this other boy and smile and talk to him about school and movie stars and popular records. He was very handsome and, she thought, not at all conceited, nothing like the way she had imagined a boy from Mount Giliad would be.

Greendale High School had several neighborhoods sending their students there. One of the most prosperous neighborhoods, before they built their own high school, was Mount Giliad. The houses all had lawns there and imitated English country homes in their entrances and roofs. They all had patches of green around them; the students of Mount Giliad were a source of wonder to the scholars from Sobaski's Stairway. They seldom mixed.

Dolly watched Dick Eastland closely. He had none of the mannerisms of a Sobaski's Stairway boy, none of the hostility, the swagger. He did not wipe his spoons with a napkin as Ike-o did before he stirred his coffee.

"You can sit anywhere in a place, can't you?" Dolly asked him. She had thought, from observing Ike-o, that all men liked to sit facing a door; it seemed sensible. That way an enemy could not come sneaking up behind a person — Ike-o made a ceremony of finding the place in a restaurant or drugstore where he would be the most comfortable.

"Anywhere you are is the place for me," Eastland replied easily.

When he casually put his arm around her he did not rest it heavily on her shoulder as Ike-o sometimes did but instead with the palm of his hand and fingers caressed her neck. Although she could not see his hand, she knew that his fingers played in the wisps of blonde hair which eluded her comb. It gave her a peculiar feeling to think that someone admired and petted and seemed to enjoy something of her's which was itself and hardly her and required nothing more from Dolly Smolcher.

No one had ever treated Dolly as kindly as Dick Eastland did. He held doors open for her and offered her cigarettes and promised her he would teach her to drive his Ford convertible.

"I have a boy friend," she told him. "He's in the army and I'm so lonely for him I'd go out with the devil just to be away from Sixth Street for a while."

"I'm not that bad, am I?"

"No," she said, "you're good looking — you look Polish."

He laughed; and it was a long time before she knew why tears came to his eyes and he choked when he looked at her. He could not stop laughing.

"That's out, mister," she said the first time he tried to feel her, sliding his hand gently up her silk-stockinged knee. They sat in his convertible, and she moved away from him roughly, staring sullenly at Sobaski's Stairway below. "I think we better go home," she said. And home was down there below Harris' Hill, street lights and window lights and people stepping into darkness and shadow, the cause of a personal pain to her because it was down there where she belonged.

"Look, Dolly," he said, "I'm sorry — I'd be foolish not to be interested in you."

She did not talk until he stopped a block away from her home. "I'm getting married," she said. "The right time for what you were doing is when a person is married."

He sat watching her as she walked away. He seemed apologetic the next day in school — he told her if it were not for his family he would make an announcement to her.

He saw her again the next Saturday night and casually

told her that he loved her and needed her desperately —
not for sex, he swore, but for someone to talk to, while his
hand slid on her knee and touched her bare thighs. He
thought a declaration of love would make it easier for her —
weren't most girls that way? Each time she went to mention Ike-o he would bend forward and kiss her. He was
himself surprised that she was that easy; he would have
been astonished to know that the event in the back of his
car was the first time for her.

"I did it," Dolly told the face in her mirror the next
morning, observing the pale face for changes, for telltale
signs of her misdeed, but the face was the same, the
body as unmarred as the day before: the sun shone and
girls and boys walked into Greendale High in the same
way as the day before, shuffling, wrestling — all the world
was the same, but Dolly Smolcher was not a virgin, and
yet the whole thing, the confused longing and fear that
Ike-o would know, was only a tiny thing inside her own
bosom. No one in the world would ever know if she did not
tell them.

"No," she said each time, "no, no, I do not love you."
But it happened anyway.

"I love only Ike-o Hartwell," she told herself.

Ike-o had thought it was so important, important
enough to hide away as a treasure not to be unveiled
until they were married, but to Dolly coming across for a
nice boy like Dick Eastland had not seemed as momentous
as Ike-o had made it sound. She did not like it or dislike it;
she had no experience with people who were kind to her.
She did it with Eastland frequently. It did not seem a

proper thing to do in a car by a four o'clock sun, but she had no objections either. Sitting at night with Eastland in a car atop Harris' Hill and gazing down at the lights of Sobaski's Stairway below was not her idea of a good time; with Ike-o yes, he would not see only the gay lights of Sobaski's Stairway. To Dick Eastland the knowledge of Sobaski's Stairway was as uncertain as a picture of Egypt in a photo magazine. She said, "I love Ike-o," to herself even while Eastland caressed her, and she knew she did not love him; but there was nothing in the mirror the next morning to show her that the thing was as important as Ike-o made it seem.

The terror did not come home to her until the night they were caught by a private detective. Eastland parked his car on Friday nights on the driveway behind one of the largest houses in Mt. Giliad; he told Dolly he knew the people of the house and they were never home on Friday nights. The private guards drove a black car. They were as silent as the night, approaching by foot while they parked a hundred yards away in the driveway. Eastland claimed he had not known the guard's intentions when he was asked to sit with another uniformed detective in a squad car. She was left alone in the crazy, dark night with hairy hands as insistent as spiders and strong as steel. He was a tobacco-stained man as old as her father, and, before the mirror at home that night, she saw the deceptive nature of the act Ike-o held in such respect. It hid its real face down inside a person and left them outside as unmarked as babies. But it was on the inside that pain grew, swelled, held a rotten party inside a person. She had thrown herself against the door of the car screaming hysterically; the private guard had not gone further but punched her to the ground and kicked her where she lay. Eastland drove her home in silence. "But I love Ike-o," she said, staring unbelievingly at her image. "I really love him." Her ribs were bruised from the kick, but the guard had not gone all the way. She was thankful; the man would have preferred the worst charges against her, he said, showing her a badge, and she was frightened enough to accede, but the screams had come from somewhere to save her. She had started to spread her legs for him but had screamed like a frightened child instead. She cried all night with a recognition that she had sinned. She was no better than her sisters. And what she wanted was someone to hold a door open for her, to buy her a pack of chewing gum, to ask her how did a classy girl like Dolly Smolcher come from Sobaski's Stairway.

Two weeks later she knew positively she was pregnant by Eastland. She had not seen him in that time, but she waited for him after school and called him away from a group of students.

"I'm in trouble, Dick," she said.

"What kind of trouble?"

"I'm pregnant."

"You're crazy — you can't be."

"I am, I am, don't tell me — I know what I'm talking about."

"Not so loud, for Christ's sake."

They stood in silence with the sun making their shadows long and angular on the high school walk and blurring them out where they crawled up on the grass. The world went on oblivious to the rotten party inside Dolly, the face no one could see: a pretty pale girl, blonde on the outside, standing silently with a textbook and waiting for the broad-shouldered boy in a white school sweater to speak.

"I haven't seen you in a while — what do you want from me?" he asked. The afternoon was long and gray; the sun slid from Dolly's vision.

"Nothing," she said, but not to him. She walked away from Greendale High School, cutting across their grass, avoiding the concrete path where the other students walked. Eastland ran after her.

"Look," he said, "I'll do anything I can for you."

"No, no," she said, "nothing."

He walked along with her, frightened. He looked into her face; he had told her to go, but her rigid attitude frightened him.

"I don't even know I'm the father," he blurted out in a desperate whisper.

She shook her head. "I don't want anything from you," she said, crossing the small wooden bridge at Linoleum Way which led to Sobaski's Stairway. He walked across with her, then stopped. He stopped and watched her walk toward Mechanic Avenue.

"Dolly!" he called uncertainly.

"Nothing," she said to herself. There was nothing outside in the world. It was all in the pain inside. Overnight, perhaps in only five minutes, Dolly Smolcher had stepped from the sunshine world of surfaces and opacity into the hidden world of suffering where a person grows up. It was not enough to say, "I love Ike-o," there was to say "nothing" and to feel nothing, vacant, numb, hurt and grown, a nothingness outside and inside too.

"I'm pregnant," she told her sister Rita.

"Golly, kid, that's rough. Do you want the name of a lady who'll help you?"

"No."

"What are you going to do?"

"Have the baby, what else?"

It was a queer way of looking at things, Rita thought.

"It's easier a lot of other ways," Rita said, "you've got a bad start having a kid. Guys are tough enough to get without a kid in the bargain. What's the soldier boy going to say?"

"How should I know?"

"Don't bite me, kid," Rita snapped back. "It ain't me going to pitch a squealer. Not until that old ring is sitting on the third finger of my left hand."

Dolly lay on the bed; she observed the flowers on the wallpaper. They had dots on them which looked like faces. Tonight she looked at the happy ones. Some were happy. Some were sad.

Rita sat on the bed and took her hand. "It's a hell of a thing," Rita said. "I know what I'm talking about. Get ahold of Ike-o — make him the father. Nine out of ten marriages started that way. You listening?"

"I love Ike-o," Dolly said.

"Well, do him a favor," Rita said.

Dolly turned over. There was nothing that happened outside in the world, only inside. Dolly wept inside. But her face was calm and hard.

"It's your funeral," Rita said.

"I'm not about to die," Dolly said. "I always wanted a kid of my own."

"Oh, boy, you got a lot to learn."

Dolly handed Rita a greeting card which had been lying on the floor near the bed. Two hearts were intertwined on it. "Ike-o sent me this," she said.

"It ain't Valentine's Day," Rita said.

"It was my birthday last week," Dolly said. "I was sixteen on Wednesday."

7

Korea, the name, the spell of retreat and cold, fascinated and frightened Ike-o Hartwell. He was not a newspaper reader ordinarily, except for the baseball scores, but he bought three different newspapers daily, reading them thoroughly by the lights in the latrine. He could see himself helpless at the first sound of gunfire, fleeing away from an Oriental enemy, running as if a street gang from Mechanic Avenue chased him.

Ike-o's hands trembled when he thought of the Korean battles and retreats, and, when the Chinese entered the fight, not the Chinks from the laundry or the disorganized cowards who ran before the Japanese when he was a kid, but the cruel, the unfearing, the deadly men wrapped in rags who won only and did not lose, Ike-o could no longer read the papers. He still bought three papers, read the scores and comics, and threw them away, as if by passing the news through his hands even without knowing what retreat had occurred, he somehow made his position better.

He lost a sweet spot as a result of the Korean War, no longer a personnel dandy, hitting his typewriter at ten and quitting at three. He could remove men's names from alternate shipping orders, quietly with no permission needed from anyone. He swaggered through his headquarters company area, a new Gedunsky, trading secrets instead of jobs with the county; he left the job uneasily. No one had declared war.

"It'll blow over in a week or two," he heard in his barracks, and repeated it every chance he could, as if saying it often enough would make it happen. "A week, two," he said confidently, assured of listeners because of his reputation as a man with sources of information, but his own orders came and he could not change them and lost his Class A pass, unlimited freedom to come and go into Washington, D.C., and went like a boy scout to live in a tent. "Meet yours truly, eagle scout Hartwell," he wrote to O. C. Gedunsky. "They got me living in a tent and eating out of a skillet they call a mess kit. Sometimes it rains and my skillet runs over. We hire a guy to bring us ham sandwiches up from the service club. They got us living in tents like boy scouts, but the service club is right over the hill. The reason I don't go myself is that they got guys standing around who will do nothing but shoot you."

The army had been a playground until the start of the Korean battles. Almost a year to the day from the time he had enlisted, the lazy, inefficient, happy-go-lucky round of beer drinking, shacking up with Southern tramps, and occasionally picking up minute scraps of paper stopped, to be replaced by a desperate cycle of continuous training.

He did not mind the new work. He was nineteen and there were reservists in the field-training company who were forty and held the efforts to a snail's pace. Ike-o jumped ditches, swung on and climbed ropes, wrestled at night in a circle by a campfire with other young men; cleaned his rifle to a high polish and his shoes to a mirror; fired his rifle, enjoying more than the report and power of the M-1 the feel of himself throwing himself on the ground with a thump, hard, honest, not worried about mud or rock or bruises. He finished the obstacle course close to first every time. Near the end of the training cycle, an officer, a West Point lieutenant, called Ike-o and another young soldier a few feet away from where Ike-o had been squatting at dinner.

"Where are you from, soldier?" he asked. Ike-o answered quickly, "Sobaski's Stairway, sir, it's a place right in Pittsburgh, Pennsylvania." "And you, soldier?" the lieutenant asked the other boy. "Brooklyn, New York, sir," the boy answered. "What's your name, soldier?" "Hartwell, sir." "And yours?" "Restino."

The lieutenant was a young man himself, with a face made thoughtful by blue eyes and slow, heavy eyelids. "You city boys make good soldiers," he said, "you're tough."

When the lieutenant had walked away from them, still apparently thoughtful, still absorbed in the matter of who was tough and who was not, Ike-o and the other boy impulsively shook hands. "Them big farm hicks ain't worth a pimple on a good soldier's ass," Restino said.

"Too dumb," Ike-o said, "too dumb, no savvy."

But he could not hide the growing fear from himself,

when the lights on the training hills went out, and night stretched out with the soldiers, when only the wind flapped the tents and every sound made Ike-o Hartwell wonder how the sounds and frost would be in Korea. Several times the idea of Korea occurred to him while he ate. He threw up his food after supper. Korea was cold and moving in his stomach. He had wanted to be brave, maybe a hero. He had hoped someday to be recognized for doing something important. But when it came to a show-down, as it had when he saw the first terrible headlines in the paper about the Chinese and read of their ferocity and Oriental contempt for life, he had stopped thinking of himself as someone who wanted to be gung-ho, someone on the side of the United States Army. As in years past, trained fine like a hunted street creature, he searched for an angle. He wanted to beat the army. He was ashamed, but he lay awake nights in his tent contriving ways to avoid duty and daydreaming about women; his arms broke out in a light rash and nightly he went alone, after lights out, and, against the medic's orders, scrubbed his arms in the shower stalls with G.I. soap. He wanted his arms to be as ugly and raw as possible; and then he developed a hope-ful stitch in his right side.

It was not a ruptured appendix as he had wished, but he was detained for a thorough examination at the post hospital for the rash on his arms. The rash began to clear up within a week; and Ike-o grimly prepared for a final medical examination, regarding it not simply as a medical evaluation which would send him back to the tents but as the first, emphatic shove toward Korea, toward de-feat, disgrace. And, in the impersonal line of men filing past the doctors, Ike-o wanted to cry out, to halt the line and the steady movement forward. He seemed to be moving toward the two medics seated on stools faster than any of the other men. The men calmly took two steps, stopped and waited. Ike-o wanted to run backward.

"Look," Ike-o said, after he had been cheerfully told his arms were healed, "look at my ankles — they're swollen up like balloons, don't that mean something?"

The captain looked at Ike-o's ankles and then slowly back at his face. "There's nothing wrong with your ankles. They're no worse than mine."

Walking in the hospital corridor back to his bed, Ike-o thought of the doctor looking from his ankles to his face, the curious pause when he looked into his eyes, narrowing his own eyes to observe Ike-o's intentions in mentioning his ankles. His ankles had seemed large to Ike-o, and he had called the doctor's attention to them, grasping for any symptom that might prolong his stay in the hospital. Ike-o laughed; he understood the doctor's concern. I sounded like a psycho, he thought bitterly, and then, I'd be better off if I was.

Then Ike-o walked through a swinging door back into the long recreation room which was used as an examination clinic for ambulatory cases. He walked quietly but directly to the front of the line.

"Captain," he said, taking the medic's arm, "you're nutty. Take another look at your own ankles. They're as big as balloons too. They can't ask us to march no more, can they?" Involuntarily the captain looked down at his ankles before he signaled for help.

Ike-o had thought the army was one big picnic for a boy
from Gardenia Street. The uniform was a passport; he had
kept it oiled and triggered like a useful weapon. It allowed
him, under the pretext of youthfulness and good spirits,
to move himself into positions where the crouching, cunning
Ike-o from up on Gardenia Street, the nobody's fool of the
whorehouses and gambling tables, could leap out as at a
fire alarm. He had arrived at a good thing as a soldier.
He bartered information for favors. He had made corporal
in six months and was promised sergeant in another three.
He was handsome and neat and scored with almost every
woman with whom he came in contact, jiving at first, talking
even of his hard life in Sobaski's Stairway, and moving in
on them, caressingly, lovingly, using his hands, his lips. He
used himself, feeling like a man with hidden qualities who
comes to the fruition of a talent. He could lie easily; others
did not seem able.

He took money, as a matter of Mechanic Avenue pride,
from a middle-aged housewife in Alexandria, like a bad
joke the wife of a traveling salesman. And from protestations
of need, of admiration, he went to domination, slapping her
hard on the buttocks some mornings, saying, "Move over,
for Christ's sake, you want to suffocate me?" He paid her
well for her gifts of money, creating drama for her in
which she cried and begged and offered to leave her husband and was punched in the cheek once and kicked in
the shins another time. Until, as happened with him, Ike-o
stood alone and fearful, the flailing fists of boyhood and an
assumed strength not enough. "Oh, God," he asked himself,
helping her to her feet, dabbing at blood at her mouth,

"Why? Why am I doing this?" They both sobbed when he broke it up, later kissing her tenderly good-by and promising to return her money. He had met her at a dinner she gave for three enlisted men at her home.

Other women had arrived and departed, another livey each weekend, hill-country girls up to spend the day in Washington, D.C., low-slung girls with hard flat feet but solid cantalouped breasts, passionate girls who wept at hill-billy music and were hot and wet and clung to him with arms made strong by men's work. There were also office girls in Washington, D.C., and lying was easy to them with fantastic love stories. These girls were so confused they were not sure of what to expect in sex. They drifted from boy friend to boy friend. They stopped at nothing to proclaim their passionate natures. But to him every woman was a tramp, except the ones he had not had. He despised the women in the offices because they needed a love story to make sex good. He tried every woman he met, thinking that the only good woman was one a man married after knowing her all of her life. That way there could be no uncertainty. That was his Dolly, never used and lying and lied to and made dirty. The rest were bums, chumps, marks if they had been born men, fit for lies and loans and contempt. Some of the office women approached the entire thing like men, asking questions of him, probing him with their heat: how did this feel? and what happened when she did this? "Hell," he thought, "that's my own damned business," and avoided those nosy and insistent women. He believed in sex Sobaski's Stairway style, that the woman was there for the man; and the proof of her stupidity was that she had so much to lose and nothing but a love story to gain.

In camp there was a fifteen-year-old who lived with a widowed father. The father was a warrant officer, and eventually Ike-o cut out the competition, perhaps eight other soldiers she slept with regularly, and saw her himself every night. He did not understand this girl or any woman. Why did they do it unless there was something bad in them?

Sneaking the Valentino under the girl's father's eyes, while he read the evening paper in the next room or played checkers with a co-worker, gave him a kind of kick that was like being on Mechanic Avenue again. But it was a kick compounded of disgust and uneasiness in the excitement.

Back home in Sobaski's Stairway, when a man spoke of a girl in a telephone booth or on a back table at a Mechanic Avenue saloon or a hump in the waiting room of the P. and L.E. train station after the last train left for town, it was like as not one of the sisters, Bertha, Rita, Irene, or Dorothey Smolcher. Ike-o found his pleasure diminished at the merest thought of them and Fats and Marg Smolcher and the slow cruise made by cars with parking lights down Sixth Avenue past the frame house. But there was always Dolly, the one made for him, the right one. He did not know why she didn't answer his letters.

She had sent him a thank-you card for a birthday card he had sent her and then nothing. He lay in his white hospital bed thinking of her and decided that her father was at the root of his trouble. He had foolishly taken a two-week furlough with his traveling salesman's wife and then had

beaten her in disgust with himself and cried and apologized
and broken it off and still longed for Dolly. He heard from
only the Catfish, one brief handwritten letter every two
weeks but no news of Dolly. Catfish Gedunsky did not
approve of the Smolchers either. After his outburst about
his ankles, Ike-o was transferred to C-9, the mental ward.

There was a steel door at the entrance to C-9 with a
small frosted window that had bars at it. A military policeman sat at the door stiffly when there were visitors and
with his feet propped against the further wall when he
was alone. In the ward was assembled a group of enlisted men who were suspected of being psychotic; they
were continually tested to find inconsistencies in their
fantasies. They were admonished that if they were found
to be faking they were liable to punishment under Article
One Hundred and Fifteen of The Articles of War, the one
set up for malingering. They were promised no punishment if they went back to duty; and some of them accepted
the offer, but most of them, like Ike-o, did not know whether
they were malingering. Of course, it had started that way.
But weird dreams of pursuit and flight, terrible headaches
came; Ike-o held onto the thought of Dolly as other men
in the ward huddled over crucifixes, believing, believing.
Later, upon discharge, unless they were hopelessly sick, all
of the men claimed to someone that they had outwitted
the army. But in the ward they communicated very little
with each other. Any man there might have been a spy.
One man crowed like a rooster at night, and some of
the men in the ward giggled, but Ike-o lay still, too anxious

about a trap to make any sign he heard. He imitated the others by day and sat sullenly looking out at the grounds outside. He talked to no one unless they spoke to him. The rash on his arms worried him into an uneasy silence. As quickly as he was told that he would probably not go to Korea it cleared up completely, leaving his arms smooth and strong again. He did not enjoy his helplessness before his own fear. He flew first at a man with a bad back a month after he was there, for no apparent reason, and then demanded to be released for duty.

He considered the episode of his fear and internment in the mental ward closed. He fought daily like a wild man, punching everyone who tried to calm him, and felt no remorse, only righteousness. "I'm ready," he roared, "let me at those Chinks." He sincerely believed he had been faking and had decided to return to duty. He was quieted with morphine; he dreamed at night of fighting and glory and blonde women with huge breasts who kissed him in the seats of a racing car when he drove through fire and air and water.

The lexicon of Sobaski's Stairway cunning, recited by the one bulb in DeAngelo's and under street lights on Mechanic Avenue, was full to bursting with heroics of men from the neighborhood who had outfoxed the army. The army was only another stiff to be outangled and used. They had feigned back injuries and lain, waited on hand and foot, by pretty nurses in expensive hospitals; they had complained of headaches and missed arduous marches; they had refused to answer questions and were sent home as stupid, not criminal, but dumb; and there was loud laughter at their obvi-

ous intelligence. In Europe a man had to shoot off his toe
to come home, in America he could put a bar of G.I. soap
under his armpit and say he had a headache. But the
army ignored Ike-o's pleas to return to duty; they did nothing with him but furnished him and the other men in C–9
with fifty new comic books a week and held inspections
and weekly told the men, through their medical captains,
that they were liable to prosecution for malingering. Ike-o's
quick rages grew more violent. He attacked a ward boy,
choking him purple, but he was not sent home. He was
ushered out of the hospital one dark morning by three
ward attendants and beaten bloody under the stately
poplars that surrounded the large building.

He became more calm, he picked no fights. He read
the comic books from front to back, reading the small print
of the advertisements for lingerie and falsies until lights
out at eight. It seemed to him he had been born in C-9.
He knew every board in the ceiling, the unique sound of
each man's breathing at night, the leaf on every tall tree
he could see through the barred window behind his bed.

One day he walked away from the porch outside the
hospital where he had been sitting. He took off his bathrobe
and pajamas and strolled in his underwear into the first
barracks he found near the hospital. He dressed himself in
a Class A private's uniform, cleaned his shoes, and went to
post headquarters, cutting across the grass quickly and
avoiding the main roads. At the post headquarters, he announced, "I want to see the commanding officer." He
knew he would be apprehended and he knew he would
be punished, but he also thought that after it was over

he would be allowed to return to duty. He was no longer afraid, he told himself, there was no terror worse than knowing a man was a coward.

He did obtain an audience with a lieutenant. "I'm not a malingerer, sir," he said. "I'm not a goldbrick. Something made me want to avoid duty but it's gone now — I only want to go back to duty. My people were Hartwells, sir. I think there was a Hartwell was an aide to General Washington. That's the kind of people I come from. Please, please, I'll be glad to go to Korea now. I couldn't help myself. You know how it is — the first thing I thought of was to break and run."

Two military policemen in a jeep returned him to C-9. He went quietly, not throwing punches; he was ready to drift, to be moved by the army. He would resist no longer.

He had one friend in C-9, a master sergeant who read books and played solitaire. He did not seem to want to talk most of the time and Ike-o respected his privacy. He avoided him even though he liked to listen to the man. The sergeant read books, he said, that were the greatest classics, but Ike-o had never heard of any of the authors in high school. He kept a fifth of whiskey under his copies of the strange books by Kafka, Dostoevsky, and Joyce. He bribed the ward boys to keep him supplied and was an object of amazement to Ike-o Hartwell. The sergeant had been in the army thirteen years, was a graduate of the University of North Carolina, and on some peculiar whim had stolen a motorboat and run it aground on the soft Potomac sands. He was caught when they found him sitting in the boat. He had made no attempt to escape. "I'm not afraid of you," he was supposed to have said to his captors. "There is no fear, only horror."

Ike-o hoped he would leave C-9 before the sergeant. He would be lonely without him; it was the knowledge that a friend sat across the room reading or playing solitaire that helped him, even though the sergeant seldom spoke. In that drawling, educated way, Ike-o decided that the sergeant was as hep as O. C. Gedunsky.

"I'm not nutty, sergeant," Ike-o told him. "I keep telling them that."

"Of course."

"Then why do they keep a sane man here?"

The sergeant shrugged his shoulders. "I don't know," he said.

"Even if I was playing at crazy at first, I mean, rubbing soap on my arms and acting dumb, does that mean that when I'm ready to go back they should say I'm really nuts?"

Sergeant Rogers thought about it. "They figure anybody who'd try what you did to buck for staying in this country has to have something wrong with him," he said.

The men in C-9 held a New Year's Eve party to celebrate the arrival of 1952. Attendance was signified by grouping themselves around the sergeant's foot locker and downing a shot from a paper cup and then passing the cup to the next man. Ike-o looked at them standing there in their army bathrobes and decided they might have been lonely men anywhere: the sergeant, half Indian with coarse black hair and something so bad eating him it twisted his mouth and made his eyes shifty; Rooster, probably a comedian in Harlem but taking his life in his hands to join their group and act normal without crowing (although he probably would make some peculiar sound and spring to the top post of his bed if an officer came); the man named Sneed, who was suspected of being a spy but was pulling lousy duty anyhow for a holiday; and Emory, who was some sort of sex maniac and would draw a picture in the air and say, "Now, wasn't that an ass," and make similar remarks on his skill in describing parts of the female anatomy in the air. Ike-o thought if it was an act with Emory then he had probably surprised himself the first few times he performed it; and Ike-o supposed that those congregated there who thought of themselves as malingering had all surprised themselves too. And before that: he would have fought someone a year ago who suggested he would try to avoid duty by feigning sickness. But now he repeated every morning at inspection, not ashamed, not caring about the curious glances, "I was malingering, sir, I wish to be punished and returned to duty." No one ever laughed when Ike-o left the inspection ranks, men standing at attention at their beds, and sat down on his bunk. "Let me out of here," he sometimes shouted. "I want to return to duty."

He felt as if he belonged at this C-9 New Year's party. He had troubles as deep as any of the men around the foot locker.

"I come a long way," Rooster said, "but I never thought I'd come this far."

"Me too," Ike-o said, and some of the others agreed.

"There are worse things can happen to a man," Sergeant Rogers said. "He could lose his self-respect."

They all looked at the floor; it was an unquiet thought.

Most of them had sacrificed that precious quality when they did not return to duty at the army's threats and urgings.

"I'd give fifty dollars to have Sophie Tucker here," Backie said, stepping into their shame and loneliness.

"Sophie Tucker!" Rooster hooted. "What you gone do with a woman that old and fat?"

"I ask you what you do with your women?"

They sang "Auld Lang Syne" and promised each other they would all keep in touch when they left the ward. That night Ike-o cried himself to sleep and Rooster did not crow.

There was an uneasiness about C-9 that the few unnatural moments of comradery did nothing to dispel. None of the men trusted each other, and there was a rumor that a medical officer, Colonel Albert C. Perkins, was coming to inspect C-9.

This Colonel Perkins had a reputation for being tough, but Ike-o did not fear him. He looked forward to explaining his case to someone new. The ward boys were happy to tell Ike-o what they knew, watching his face as payment back for the indignity of emptying bedpans and feeding aspirins to the creeps at three in the morning. Colonel Perkins was the answer to their prayers; he was the ultimate threat, one man tougher than anyone else, heartless, soulless, the army's power and cold, pitiless sword hanging overhead. No matter what happened, things would be worse after Colonel Perkins left. The ward boys said the colonel believed everyone claiming mental illness was a coward. He was supposed to have said that he'd take an able-bodied nut to a sickly sane man anytime. He said enemy cannons didn't know the difference, the ward boy repeated. The threat of the colonel's impending visit made most of the men tremble, but Ike-o was jubilant for the first time in months. He would look the colonel squarely in the eye and say "Sir, I wish to be returned to duty. I am ready to take my punishment." Anything was better than C-9. But eventually he succumbed. He trembled with fear, sweating cold at night under blankets, at the thought of Colonel Perkins.

He brought his disturbed feelings across the room to Sergeant Rogers. He had started to dream of Colonel Perkins. He did not want to join the general terror in the ward, but the impending visit had become a vision of the end of the world to Ike-o. If fire and brimstone had rained down the three weeks they sat and waited for Colonel Perkins Ike-o would not have been shocked. He had stopped a Captain Cunningham in the corridor the day before; the waiting, the rumors, the fear had grown stronger while Ike-o tried to subdue them, telling himself that honesty was on his side, he had nothing to fear.

"Please, sir," Ike-o said, "let me go back to duty."

"You can just tell your troubles to Colonel Perkins," the captain said, and roared with knowing laughter, a sergeant with him in a white technician's tunic joining in. "He's very sympathetic."

"Watch yourself," the sergeant said, stepping between Ike-o and the captain, sensing Ike-o's angry mood, and then calling him back to salute the officer before he left.

Sergeant Rogers kept his finger on a place in the book

he was reading. His face twitched while he listened. He finally nodded when he was sure Ike-o was through; there was no laughter in his face, none of the mockery of C-9.

"What kind of nut house is the whole damned army?" Ike-o demanded.

"It takes all kinds," Sergeant Rogers said. "Do saints ever carry rifles? — I know some saints went ashore at Anzio."

"Is this crazy?" Ike-o asked. "Before this nut ward, I liked the army, I wanted to do good, I ain't a coward by reason. I guess nobody is, but I really wanted to fight somebody for the country. When it came to fighting, I mean, a real fight in Korea, I turned so yellow my arms broke out and I got a headache."

"Some people are fighters, others are not."

"Why me? Why couldn't I be a fighter if that's what I thought I wanted?"

"You didn't have the equipment. There's something a person has to have in order to do a specific thing. You don't have the thing to be a fighter, I mean a soldier, there's other kinds of fighters."

"Sergeant, can I ask you something personal?"

"Go ahead, I'm not saying I'll answer truthfully."

"If you don't like the army, why have you stayed in all these years?"

Sergeant Rogers' mouth stopped twitching while he grinned. "I said it's a crazy setup. I didn't say I didn't like it," he said. "Don't forget on my service record it says 'screwball.'"

"You're kidding me."

"A little bit, not altogether. Armies are necessary, Ike-o, but that doesn't make them sane or logical or even useful except if somebody else's army wants to molest your country."

Ike-o said, "I wish I were dead."

"That's probably worse yet," Sergeant Rogers said. "You understand, that's my opinion."

Ike-o laughed. "You do me good, sergeant."

"Here, kid," Sergeant Rogers said, leaning on an elbow and holding up a book he had been reading. He did not offer the book to Ike-o but shook it as a demonstration. "This guy was the greatest horror writer in the world until the mass grave spirit came out in mankind. This man's name is Dostoevsky, he was a Russian that didn't like the Czar, had a little salt blown in his butt, and decided he did like the Czar after all. He was sent out to be shot one day. They even had the blindfold adjusted — instead of shooting him they called the whole thing off, it was a trick of the Czar's to harass his prisoners. What do you think of that horrible story?"

Ike-o did not know what to say; Sergeant Rogers was excited. He swung his legs over the side of his bunk and sat glaring at Ike-o with eyes that would not stop moving. "Well?" he asked. "What do you think of that horrible story?"

"I don't know what to say," Ike-o admitted.

"You're damned right you don't," Sergeant Rogers said, "because, for one thing, there's more horror goes on every day that passes for ordinary living than Dostoevsky could have seen in a lifetime. Listen, I was in Berlin right after the war ended with the Krauts. I'll tell you some horror stories. You take all the things mankind has been writing down and preserving as examples of the terrible things can happen if the madmen take over, they ain't a whisper to the stories you could hear in any German cellar. Believe me, buddy, there were four million innocent people killed over there. That's the greatest horror story of all time. Don't tell me about Perkins or Dostoevsky and his blindfold and Czar with special boots to kick the peasants. Today you have to know your multiplication tables to keep tabs on horror. And every one of the four million suffered like Dostoevsky, even if they weren't able to write about it as well. What's Perkins going to do to you life hasn't already done?"

Ike-o's head began to hurt. He did not know what to answer Sergeant Rogers, he could think of nothing that would not make him sound like a fool.

"Do you know what a woman's body is?" Sergeant Rogers asked abruptly.

The man's face ticked so violently Ike-o was afraid he was going to be forced to call a ward boy. He was frightened even to glance toward the door. "I guess I slept with a few women," Ike-o said.

"That ain't what I mean," Rogers said. "I'm talking about how a woman's body functions, how it takes itself and prepares like a garden and creates in its depth life and babies. If you haven't thought of that, soldier, you haven't turned over in your sleep yet. You're two hours away from reveille. Don't talk to me about fear."

"Look," Ike-o said quietly, "we're disturbing some of the

other guys." But it was not true; the men in the ward lay bent on their elbows or on their backs and feigned the most complete indifference. Yet Ike-o knew there was not one man who was not listening.

"I met a girl in Berlin," Rogers said, "she was sixteen, seventeen then, a hustler since maybe ten, they were all hustlers. She was only seven when the Germans took her family to a camp for scientific experiments. You know what the Germans did with women, what they did with those beautiful instruments for making life? — They'd tell the women every morning they'd be gassed that day. You know how systematic they are, every day they'd take the time to type out certain women's names to make them think that at such-and-such a time they were going to be dumped in a gas oven. And you know their reason? — They were checking the women's menstrual period to see the effect of fear on it. That wasn't happening to a handful of prisoners up in Siberia somewhere the same time we still had slaves in the United States; that was happening to hundreds of women in the most civilized part of the world while, not ten miles away, Heinies were drinking beer and saving their ration stamps to have enough for a big Sunday dinner." He laughed wildly, pounding himself on the leg with his book. "See, on a comparable basis," he said, "the Czar was a good fellow, he never claimed he was doing his cruelty to benefit mankind."

"I get what you're driving at now."

"No, Ike-o, you don't. There's a point past which the mind can't go, and what happened to the four million people and every day in Russia right now is something the mind just can't take in. You can't even understand horror to begin with unless you practice. I been practicing and I can't do it. One toothache in my head supersedes a thousand nice old Chinamen shot down in cold blood." He lay back in his bed. "Go back to your bunk, kid," he said. "I ain't mad at nobody. I ain't angry. In six years I don't even remember the horror I used to feel. I ain't afraid either — *c'est la vie*, like the French say."

He opened this book by Dostoevsky. "This guy should be alive today. Europe would crush him. Take him for a walk in the hospital corridor, huh, kid?"

Ike-o went back to his bunk and sat on the edge and looked at the sergeant from across the room as if he would understand him better by additional distance. He lay back with his secret pain and thought that soon something would come of the interview with Perkins; but nothing happened in the ward for two days, except for the incident when Backie refused to stand inspection and hid under his bed and was dragged out and held at attention by two corporals. His back was straight when they held him but went immediately into its familiar stoop the minute he was released.

The trees outside dripped rain and the remnants of snow that lingered in the leaden sky. In the Southern climate the snow did not stay on the ground. It melted as if the earth itself, inside Virginia, was boiling the way Ike-o's head was. He watched the sleet and waited.

Two days before the inspection by Colonel Perkins he was awakened at midnight and walked by a civilian from the Red Cross out to the corridor where the M.P. sat with his feet propped against the wall. The corridor was cold with that Southern damp. Old soldiers said it had been the slowest spring in coming they could remember. The man from the Red Cross shivered; he was tired and smelled of whiskey. He had been brought away from a party on the post to bring the message.

He informed Ike-o that the Red Cross on the post had received a telegram from their office in Greendale, Pennsylvania. His father, Charles Morgan Hartwell, had succumbed to pneumonia the previous day. He told Ike-o that if he would permit a police guard, the Red Cross could get him a pass to go home for the funeral. Ike-o thought for a short moment and said, "Forget it. Thanks." The man from the Red Cross hurried away. Ike-o returned to his bunk alone.

He lay the long night listening to the other men in the ward snoring and whimpering in their sleep. Morning did not come quickly. He did not weep but felt sad and at the same time as if a pressure had been removed from inside his chest. There was one person less then in a town dump far away called Sobaski's Stairway: another chair vacant in DeAngelo's, one more place on the bar in Rebecca Goldstein's. How Charlie Hartwell had been a beam of sunlight to the boy Ike-o! — There had been none of the alley shadows bold enough to poke forward their dark fingers in the places where he strutted, the smoky rooms where he talked. The ground was cold and damp where he would lay in the short spring; and there would be no one to listen to him, no one but the night wind to laugh and find him funny. He would turn to ashes, his grimaces and jigging unnoticed by the distant stars. There would not even remain the boy's love of the father. They had been two strangers in a foolish affection a long time ago.

One less bully, one less drunkard, the world poorer for one less loudmouth and pudgy little redheaded man with bad kidneys in a stolen overcoat: Good-by, Father.

Oh, sleep well, Yolanda.

Listen, God, bless her; put a thing on her to make her know that trouble is gone from her life. Kid her, tell her everything's going to be okay now. Sleep tight, Yolanda, there ain't forty thieves abroad to rob you or army rats gnawing at your boy. There's one thing better in the world tonight. Charlie Hartwell is dead. When dawn came in at the barred windows it was again wet and gray. The beautiful high trees that lined the approaches and walks to the hospital stood stark but blurred with the fine rain and a morning fog. Ike-o watched the poplars through the bars as they grew more black and distinct with daylight.

"Possibly I was malingering, sir," Ike-o said, exactly as he had planned, "but I am ready for my punishment. Please, sir, I wish to be returned to duty."

The colonel had proven to be human, a spare man with a scraggly mustache and blue-veined hands, a wrinkled man whose face and hands seemed to be held together by his crisp uniform. He walked slowly through the ranks and did not seem unkind. He talked so quietly that the inmates, spaced ten feet apart, could not hear what he said to the man next to them. They stood at attention at their foot lockers.

"We still face a deadly enemy in Korea, Corporal Hart-well," the colonel said quietly. "Can we count on your help?"

"Yes, sir, but my enlistment runs out in about eight months' time, counting the forty-five days of furlough time I've accumulated." He stood at ease, not looking at Colonel Perkins but out to where grass grew green and smooth.

Colonel Perkins studied him, stroking with two long fingers his sparse mustache. He said, "We would no sooner get you to Korea then we'd have to bring you back. Is that the point?"

"Yes, sir," Ike-o said.

Colonel Perkins smiled gently behind his fingers. "You are sure, Corporal Hartwell, that you are well enough to return to duty?" he asked, barely audible, but smiling.

Ike-o said, "Yes, sir, I am."

"Make a note of that, sergeant," Colonel Perkins said, as if the information had only penetrated to the core of the army's understanding at that moment and had not been stated every day by Ike-o for months. A white tunicked non-com noted something on a paper attached to a clipboard.

Under Colonel Perkins' eyebrows there was no anger for Ike-o, scarcely a knowledge of him. Ike-o breathed faster, thinking of release, of freedom. "Thank you, sir," he said.

"You will serve, of course, the seven months and twenty-three days you've spent in our hotel up here," Colonel Perkins said, still smiling, but now Ike-o saw the bitterness to the wrinkled face, the smile an effect of false teeth, and portions of the weak mustache that obscured the upper lip. "That gives you," the colonel said, "a total of fifteen months more to make a man of yourself."

"No," Ike-o said, "no," choking not at the sentence but at the colonel's power and his helplessness, at the ability of a man to impose perhaps death and cowardice on someone else, someone who stood choking and trembling in army carpet slippers. Ike-o controlled the helplessness; he pulled in his stomach and pushed back his shoulders. He stood at a rigid attention. He felt for the first time in a long while a soldier.

"At ease," the colonel said, sensing he was being used by the rigid posture of the boy. "At ease, I said."

When Ike-o remained at a stiff attention, the colonel shouted, "As God is my witness, you'll be in Korea before the month is up, Corporal Hartwell."

The solemn departing procession mocked him, death without seeing Dolly or his mother again, white walls and blank faces and even Sergeant Rogers too preoccupied to look at him that day or the next or the long, white day after that. The days were dreamlike in their isolation. Ike-o felt that it was someone else being examined, prodded, being given shots to go overseas. Only the name Korea remained as real.

On a Saturday morning he knew that it was his last inspection in C-9, but not freedom waiting, Korea. Only the inside of his boiling head was his; he could make out that the inspecting officer was Colonel Perkins, white retinue following him, and nothing more complicated except that clipped and rolling grass offered no comfort, blank inmate faces across the aisle might have been those of other Ike-o Hartwells. He did not recognize his individual enemy until the final terror of dying in Korea burst on him, and then he saw everything, but differently, larger, smaller, brighter, nearer, farther. Oddly, he watched himself with a microscopic perfection too in those moments when his daze lifted and clarity and anger took its place.

He saw Perkins' hunched back. The colonel stood swaying at the head of a flight of stairs. He saw himself watching the khaki back and saw Ike-o Hartwell dispatching himself from the other inmates lined up along their beds like their own shoes or foot lockers and walking in his carpet slippers to the hunched back with the eagle on the shoulder and not knowing what he was going to do; and then, in mystery and horror, saw the colonel tumbled, a skinny windmill of khaki legs and arms, down the stairs, and realized that he had shoved him and knew irrevocably he had kissed good-by his clean discharge.

"I knew somehow something like this would happen to me," he said boldly to the intern who handcuffed him to his metal hospital bed. "They made jails for guys like me." Crouched on the wooden floor, he saw the world around him seemingly reduced, in his moment of clarity, to all of the hungers and terrors that dwelled in mankind. Fear, hatred, he saw them in the interns who held him flat; and brutality and slavery, they were almost smells on the non-coms who roughly slapped him and instinctively looked about for praise. He saw cowardice, as abstract and as nameless as goose pimples; it rippled around the ward as if Ike-o had been a huge rock tossed into a white, placid lake. The men looked away, finding the poplars outside the windows easier to take than the man struggling on the floor.

But Ike-o said, "Goddamn you!" not to any of them. He knew these men. He understood the abstract horrors they represented. He said, "Goddamn you!" reaching at first to bite his hand and then snarling up at him, to Sergeant Rogers, whose Indian face he saw that day for the last time in his life. He had spoiled Ike-o's perfect understanding, his control and anger. Ike-o's hatred could not be pure with such a man present. Why was there always one chump? Why did he cradle Ike-o's head in his arms and say, "Easy, easy, man, don't be afraid." It was impossible to hate the world when there appeared one person with kindness and no percentage. The sergeant stroked Ike-o's head and in the other hand carried an open switch blade to ward off the circling non-coms.

"Goddamn you!" Ike-o cried, "you're no better than the rest of them. Damn you! Damn you!" But Ike-o knew better, however, and loved life even while he wished he were dead. The sergeant said, "Easy, easy, Ike-o," stroking his head smoothly, but the courage left Ike-o as he knelt on the floor near the bed. By the time the military police came to take him he was screaming incoherently and biting the stainless steel handcuffs that held him.

Dolly accepted the telegram from her father in the lobby of the office building where she worked. It was her lunch hour and she waited for her father to leave before she opened the telegram, but she knew he already knew the contents. He was waiting for her reaction. Joy lit up Fats Smolcher's eyes. "Imagine that telegram kid finding me at Rebecca Goldstein's," he said. "I wasn't in there ten minutes when he came and found me. Another five and he would have missed me." Dolly tore open the telegram. "It's from Ike-o," she said. "He'll be home on Monday. He's discharged." Fats had not closed the envelope flap as carefully as usual; the envelope had obviously been opened.

"Well, well," Fats said, "I think that's good news."

"I'm not going to lie to him," Dolly said.

Fats looked around the lobby; he found it hard to conceal his rage. His face became red. "You ain't got no choice," he whispered.

8

Ike-o peered into the late afternoon fog to reaffirm the scene. The Smolchers' little frame house on Sixth Street was gone, and Catfish Gedunsky's house on Second Street was just as invisible.

Ike-o inhaled early dusk on Mechanic Avenue with a sense of anticipation. He stood squarely in his paratrooper boots at the corner of Second Avenue and Mechanic Avenue and breathed in happiness as well as brick dust with every breath. First Avenue still remained, there were two churches there whose congregations had failed appeals: but Second, Third, Fourth, Fifth, and Sixth Streets, along with the alley tributaries of Our Way, Castle Road, Henderson Way, and McCully Place, were not.

Where they had been was a huge torn-up field of piled rubble, bricks, and lumber, and a rickety low wooden fence ran around the entire five-block area.

Aching as if he had been in a fight the night before, still stiff from the bus ride home, Ike-o had sought information about Dolly. He had stopped in every place where Fats Smolcher was known, turning down narrow alleys dark even with the afternoon sunlight, inquiring in cellar poolrooms and barbershops, and knocking gingerly at first, then louder as the morning wore on, at the heavy oak doors of lone prostitutes. He had finally uncovered at the Mechanic Avenue Police Station his first real hint that would help him locate one of the missing Smolchers.

An uneasiness came into Ike-o's good feelings: so it was happening, Sobaski's Stairway — the blighted business area on Mechanic Avenue fit only for store-front religions and gypsies, saloons, pawnshops, poolrooms, and postage stamp delicatessens, and the perennially condemned tenements — was being decimated. But Sobaski's Stairway was not a layed-out corpse yet. Over there, at Seventh Street and Mechanic Avenue, there started the same forest of fire escapes and amusement park posters, and clean wash hung from the windows of tenements.

Ike-o strolled happily again up Mechanic Avenue through uneven rows of dark milk-box loafers and orange-crate humbugs. He smelled yesterday's garbage on the afternoon fog and listened to the sound his boots made thumping on the old cracked sidewalk. He had bought the paratrooper boots, guaranteed to be new, in a pawnshop in Baltimore on his way home; and the uniform he wore, with the Washington monument insignia sewn on his shoulder, he had assembled in an army surplus store in Baltimore too. It did not seem right to him, damned dishonorable discharge or not, not to be wearing on his return home to Sobaski's Stairway a crisp, well-tailored army uniform. The paratrooper boots had been bought as an afterthought; his uniform did not seem complete without them.

He walked heavily, feeling strong in the late spring heat. He wore an army regulation tie and large, smoked aviator's sunglasses with golden rims. He laughed for no particular reason but the feeling of comfort in sights familiar to his eyes.

He had whiskeyed and lied his way up Mechanic Avenue that afternoon, postponing going home after leaving each place, leaning forward avidly across each new bar to hear of his particular friends. Where he was recognized as the late Charlie Hartwell's son he had been given free drinks and asked to tell about his time in the army. He talked. He had become slightly drunk on the returned hero's free whiskey and the excitement of his own stories.

He told the people he met that he had been a paratrooper, standing on doorsteps or leaning on bars, retold many times of his fifty-eight jumps from transport planes. He was congratulated, becoming drunker in each place. He promised himself that each place was the last. He talked on; he lived the excitement of his fantasies. It was good to be brave, bold, fearless. It was not Ike-o Hartwell who had put in two months in an army stockade, moody behind barbed wire, marching to the cadence of men who carried shotguns. It was someone else who stood in his shorts for a four o'clock roll call in the cold Virginia morning and was teased and tormented by prison guards. Who it was he did not remember. He recognized only the hero who had come home, the tough city boy.

Before Miss Fireman's Social Center, leaning against a pole for support, he stopped to rest, alone with his implausible lies. The night air made him dizzy. Miss Fireman's place was solid in a Mechanic Avenue that seemed unreal with vacant lots and weeds growing along the sidewalks. He knew this happy place of Miss Fireman's, a building that was home itself to him, all the good feelings of return and comfort.

Miss Fireman's building was not much different from the other buildings on Mechanic Avenue, but there was a cleanness, a sense of love and care to it. The plate-glass window of the poolroom had been replaced by large glass doors in the front. Two trees stood on the pavement before the place. Shrubbery, small trees, and trimmed bushes lined the entrance, and over the doors in neat, correct lettering was a bronze sign: The Sarah J. Fireman Center, Hot Showers, Nine to Five.

All the hot showers she allowed me, Ike-o thought, weren't enough to clean up this kid; I paid her back for her confidence. He had not written Miss Fireman in two years because he had not known what to say. She could have been dead for all the rat Ike-o Hartwell had cared.

There was no passing stranger to whom he could shout, no sound, as happened occasionally on Mechanic Avenue. It was quiet and warm and purple. Yet there was a feeling that needed to be said, whether there were people or not to hear. "I never did anything right in my life," Ike-o shouted into the quiet darkness.

Miss Fireman's illness weighed heavily on Ike-o. He could not have been sorrier for her if he had caused her lungs to become infected; he saw her building through tears and blinked them away. He had a mission. He knew where there was a link to finding Dolly Smolcher. He kicked a metal pole in passing; he kicked hard and felt nothing in his own foot through the deadly boot but heard a dull hollow whang like pain from the pole.

In an afternoon of hearing tales of decline, sickness, and disappearances from the diminishing Sobaski's Stairway, he had finally thought to ask of Fats Smolcher not among prostitutes or in the bars of Mechanic Avenue where he was remembered largely as an elephantine figure sprawled asleep in a back booth, but in the Number Two Police Station on Mechanic. The desk sergeant knew him. "He's living with an old lady named Emma Carnavan out in her bus out Fifteenth Street. We locked them both up for disorderly conduct a week ago."

Ike-o breathed in his air deeply, smelling again yesterday's garbage, old sweat, and brick dust. His one link to Dolly Smolcher lay beyond the decrepit stairway, out past the rows of rusted orange gondolas and yellow baked mounds. The worked-out soft coal mines of Greendale sat in a gloom as perpetual as that of a barren, untended cemetery. Ike-o squinted his eyes, looking out toward the rolling brown mounds as if he expected her to appear there, a quick burst of golden hair and slim, swaying carriage.

He followed a narrow path. Past Fifteenth Street the path twinkled with broken whiskey bottles and beer caps. His boots made dull thumping sounds where the clay of the path was hard.

The bus crouched near a bankrupt laundry where the brush was thickest and garbage lay heavy in any rut in the clay. The old red brick building was a shell. Inside the wooden floors were crumbled and charred where generations of bums had done their cooking. Periodically in the old days the police had invaded the place and arrested a score of nesting vagrants, but in a week's time it bustled again with cooking fumes and the sweet scent of cheap wine and marijuana. Emma Carnavan's bus huddled against the shaggy laundry like a dirty little right-angled chick against a specious mother hen. It was a place of desolation and emptiness. Ike-o shuddered to think of Dolly wandering around out on these dunes. There was no other place where he could begin searching for her except in this used-up, dead patch of Sobaski's Stairway. The Smolchers had no other home. Marg had run off with a cousin to Uniontown, Pennsylvania, and left her spoils, two toddling children and three hundred pounds of Thaddeus Smolcher, to Emma Carnavan.

Ike-o walked around the bus once, listening. The bus was older than he was: doors sagging and sealed with rags, tires skinny and bald and useless, a hood accordianed back to show prowlers that there was nothing under it to steal. The entire motor was gone.

The bus had been painted green, and there were white curtains on the windows. At the rear emergency door window a five-foot chimney made its broken-backed way up, and on the front door lettered in black was the word "WELCOME."

"Hello," Ike-o called boldly.

Emma Carnavan came to a window. She wore a white rag on her head like a wounded soldier. "You beat it, soldier," she screamed, "or I'll call a cop."

"Where can I find Dolly Smolcher?" he asked through the window.

"Miss Uppity-up! She ain't here."

"Does she ever come here?" Ike-o asked. "Would you know her address?"

"I should have known why you was snooping around here," Emma Carnavan said. Her face was white and wrinkled, except for the tip of her nose, which was a bright red. She spat when she talked. "Let me tell you something, soldier, Fats is happier now than he been in his whole life. He comes and goes and I give him the honor due a fine man like him. We sing till daylight some mornings. There ain't nobody, you or that fancy daughter of his, going to break it up either. Emma Carnavan got her ways, by God, she does." She picked up a heavy bread knife from the table and showed it to him at the window glass. "I been living by myself for twenty-one years now, not counting the four months I was married, and I can take care of Emma. And I don't mean from just some old bum creeping around here at night, I mean I'll take care of anyone trying to take my Teddy away." She shook the knife at Ike-o. "I'll carve up like a sausage that pretty face on his Miss Uppity-up she comes around here looking like the cat pissed in her pajamas."

"I don't mean you any trouble," Ike-o said. "I just got home from the army today. I'm just looking for Dolly."

"It was the best thing happened to Fats, kiddo," she

screeched. "That man needed someone to straighten him out, he was going straight to hell with that whore. Teddy's got himself a job baking now — ain't that something? — he went into the trades at his age. You ought to see the bread and cakes he brings home at night. Him and me sit here till two in the morning many a night cutting our teeth on them Danishes he stuffs into his shirt. Wash it down with honest to God gin, you want some?" She opened up a window of the bus and reached under a curtained table and snatched out a half bottle of gin. She pulled out the cork with her teeth, swigged, said, "Ah," and offered the bottle through the window to Ike-o. He waved it away.

Emma took another swig and belched. "You're the first come to visit Fats in a while, excepting for his daughter," she said. "A person would think I run off with my cousin instead of Marg Smolcher the way people looks at me. Hell, I ain't so old I can't please a man, am I, kiddo?" Ike-o shook his head no.

"I ain't no blooming violet," she said, "I know a thing or two about men. I was married once, I got the certificate to prove it. Cuban fellow. They ain't niggers, you know, they're white as you and me."

"When's Fats get home?" Ike-o asked, trying to grasp at Dolly through him.

"I can't say for sure," she said, wiping her hands on her dress. "Some nights he don't come home, some nights he does. Kiddo, Fat says he ain't never had as much fun as here on my bus with me. Goddamn, we sing till daylight the mood comes on us. I sing Fat an Irish song and he sings me one in Polish. Then we gets together on some of the good old American ones like "I Want a Girl," "Let Me Call You Sweetheart," "China Doll." She leaned far out of the window, balanced on white, baby-soft arms.

"I want a girl-rul, just like the girl who married dear old dad," she sang out. She stopped at his movement. "Where the hell are you going?" she asked.

"You sing good," he said, "but I ain't been home yet. I wanted to find Dolly first."

"This is her day off, she takes Fats' two kids out all day. The rest of the week I watch them. She comes here every night, nine, ten o'clock I can expect her. She takes the kids with her every night like I wasn't good enough to bed them down. I watch them by day while she works but I got to turn them over to her at night, Fats' orders. Dresses herself up like a man so no one'll grab her goodies out here and comes out to my bus to snoop, pretending she's picking them kids up is all. I know her reason, she's trying to break Fats and me up. Well, she ain't going to do it. You hear, soldier? she ain't."

"Yeah, yeah," Ike-o said, "go soak your head, you old drunk." He moved away quickly from the clearing before the old woman could throw something. Sure, good old Fats could sing the Polish songs, snoring, legs outstretched, while an agile and quiet girl friend could reach into a hip pocket and pull out the new baker's cashed pay check. Maybe Emma did need him for some mysterious love, Ike-o snorted. Maybe pigs did fly.

He took the rough path back to Mechanic Avenue, thinking there wasn't a person who lived in Sobaski's Stairway who did not have his hand out or in someone's pocket. The anger, the malice! He stopped in Rebecca Goldstein's for a beer, but he could not shake off the heat and the leaden quality to the night. Life seemed to stretch forward endlessly as if a true night or a fresh morning would never come and he would be embroiled for years in this torpid June day of red brick dust heavy on the air. The part of Mechanic Avenue still standing looked the same to him as he walked to 432 Gardenia Street — the buildings still as dilapidated and crumbling, and there was the same furtive attitude about the people in the street, even by a clear spring night. Everybody you ever saw on Mechanic Avenue, Ike-o thought, was hustling a body, bootleg moon, or numbers, or else was in the market for a drunk to roll, an old man with a store to rob, or a sure proposition of some kind.

The shadows and neon lights from Sobaski's Stairway blended on the upstairs window at 432 Gardenia Street to make it possible for a person to be sitting there unobserved. Ike-o shuddered, and thought it strange that there was no more of the tubby Charlie Hartwell's dreams at that window or anger or even the happiness he seemed to know standing there above Sobaski's Stairway. Green had been painted over brown, and gray over that, and something else over that until the wooden framework of the tenement was the neutral color of reptiles or rodents. All of the other buildings were the same shade. They were painted over until one place could have been another in the embrace of the equalizing gray over brown over green. But this one place had been some kind of home; this place he knew.

"Isaac?" the woman asked. "I left the door open for you. Isaac, is it you?"

"You shouldn't have," Ike-o said.

His mother had become softer and whiter since he had seen her last. And around the colors in her eyes had formed two cataracts, but she did not seem to have trouble seeing him. She heaved herself upward from the unmade bed where she sat.

"Is it really you, Isaac?" she asked.

She had become more unkempt since the night he had seen her last at the train station. She wore the same ill-fitting yellow commencement dress. He enfolded his mother in his arms and held her great bulk close and kissed her. He pressed his lips to her forehead and did not release her. She held him tightly, weeping softly. "Isaac, Isaac, Isaac, you come home at last."

Somewhere in his head there existed the words he would say if he knew them exactly. They choked him. Maybe there really were no words, only thoughts of pity and love never meant to be put into words.

"I'm here for good, Ma," he said, "there ain't nowhere I want to be but home. I'm not ever going away again." He could not stop his own bitter, tender tears. "Ma, I missed you."

The dead rustle with a window blind and clear their throats to speak above a streetcar's grind. Ike-o's room is dark with memories. Those words, those plots against the pompous little man with red hair by the neighbors, all the painful twisted extremities of his fancied importance and real failure were still in the room a year after he was dead.

Except for a shadow or two at the window he might have been standing there lost in some daydream.

"I never heard it the army don't let a boy come home for his papa's funeral," Yolanda called. "It don't seem right the army shouldn't have feelings for a person."

"I was a paratrooper," Ike-o shouted through the apartment's one door. "They're different than the army."

Ike-o looked down at the street below and then looked again into the shadows on the far side. It seemed to him that a girl stood there, a slim blonde girl who did not move but appeared to be standing there and observing him as motionlessly as he watched. "It's Dolly," he said to himself, and it seemed entirely logical that she had received his telegram and had come to stand below his window, too shy to intrude. He ran past the startled woman, down the steps heavily, and out into the street.

There was not even an object or an unusual shadow where he thought Dolly had stood; there was only the flat blackness that always lay on the doorways of Gardenia Street. He stood alone on the street, then turned and came back to his house, walking slowly back up the steps.

"I thought I saw someone I knew," Ike-o said.

He pushed away a piece of cellophane-wrapped "Delicious Angel's Food Cake" which his mother shoved at him. It looked like a wet sponge. "I don't want anything, thanks," he said. "You eat the cake — I ate."

"You was no more in the paratroops than I was," Yolanda said.

"I was so," Ike-o said. "What are you trying to do?"

"Is that so?" his mother asked. "Pour me one of them

Seven-ups, Isaac. So my little boy was a paratrooper? — my, your daddy would have been proud to know it. He kept saying you was in jail, Isaac, you know how quick he was to think the worst of someone, God rest his soul." She wept softly to herself. "I wish he'd never gone — he kept food on the table and clean sheets on the bed — depression, hard times, bad luck, he took care of us through it all."

"He never murdered you if that's what you mean," Ike-o said, and was astonished at the violence of her response.

"Shut up that talk about murder," she shouted. "Who are you to come here talking about murder? You damned jailbird."

"Calm down," Ike-o said.

She gulped the soft drink and belched quietly. She wiped her small mouth with the back of her hand. "I have human sense," Yolanda said. "I know there ain't one paratrooper so important to the United States they can't let him come home to see a dead father."

"For heaven's sake," Ike-o cried, "if they let one man go they'd have to let them all go at any little excuse. You don't have any idea of the way the army was after that sneak punch in Korea."

"Tell it to Sweeney," Yolanda said.

"It's true," Ike-o snarled, knowing that he had not deceived her, "it's true, every word."

Yolanda rocked from side to side. "You broke the heart of the only man who cared for you," she said. "You broke his heart, going to jail and not sending us one letter, and that poor man waiting downstairs by the mailbox and worrying himself to death because of your meanness. I never

seen the poor soul drink so much as when he was worried
about his son. 'My baby boy,' he called you that last
week."

"I ain't going to hear you make a saint out of that
bastard," Ike-o cried.

"He died like a fish, the poor soul, struggling up there
in the hospital without a friend but me and Fats," Yolanda
said. "There wasn't even enough air for him them last
two days, he couldn't breathe; I didn't have the strength
in my hands to squeeze his fingers enough. At the minute
before he died he closed his eyes and took an intern's hand
and said, 'My baby Ike-o, I knew you'd come home to see
Daddy.'"

"Ma, don't do this."

"There's one thing more I want from you, Isaac," she
said. "I ain't asking anything for myself."

"You know I'd do anything, Ma," he said.

She turned her white eyes toward him.

"The first thing," she said, "now you're home, is to get
a tombstone for Papa. The part where he lays is over a
hill away from the other graves. His insurance was just
enough to dig a hole in the ground and to shovel him in.
Poor Papa, he lays off to the side away from the other
graves. Maybe they ain't ever going to plant trees there
for the price I paid."

"That's sad," Ike-o said, "that's very sad, Ma."

"Charlie can't rest until we give him a real grave," Yolanda
continued, "with a tombstone. I ain't going to let hard
luck follow him in death like it did in life."

Ike-o nodded his head emphatically at the white eyes.
"That's right," he said.

"It costs plenty," his mother said. "Believe me, I know. We been planting Stanacheks in the ground for a long time. The ground is full of our people, I know."

Ike-o asked angrily, "What's the difference what it costs? I'm good for it. If I say I'll do it, I'll do it."

"A promise to a mother," she said, "is like a promise to God. We owe it to Daddy."

"I know, I know."

Ike-o went and lay across the bed in the room where the neon light from Pop's Cut-rate on Mechanic bounced to the windows across the street, blinked through the night, and second by second turned his own window pink, then black, then pink again. He turned on his radio; the tubes lit the room and dance music came on. It's a long life, he thought.

He had crouched on this bed thousands of times, escaping into the radio from the chaotic, cruel world of Charlie Hartwell, and now after his death he still came here to avoid him with dance music. He rolled over to watch the neon lights' signals. They might have been a code: Charlie lives, Charlie lives, Charlie lives. Pop's Cut-rate, world's champion seller of Blue Ointment, douche bags, and hair straightener, was going to be torn down soon, it was in the path of the redevelopment. Ike-o hoped that there was an end somewhere to his old man.

"Good night, Ma," he called, "don't worry, I'll take care of everything."

She came to stand at his door, blocking the doorway but for two dim rays from behind her that shone over her shoulders. Her features were as flat and black as the night surrounding the neon lights outside.

"I wish I could get it on paper," she said. "I'd put you back in jail you don't keep your promise."

"Okay, I'll do it," he said, and found himself waking in his own room four hundred miles from the stockade and the mental ward, mumbling, "I want to go back to duty, sir." He pulled his covers close around himself, thinking that now he had the memory of Colonel Perkins to pursue him too. He had not been asleep an hour; he turned on his radio, feeling home, realizing it in the size of his bed and sounds in the Sobaski's Stairway night. He heard footsteps on concrete and far away a streetcar and somewhere a water faucet dripping. The city noises had the familiarity and natural rhythms of crickets or birds. Ike-o listened, becoming calmer as he stretched and listened. He thought that grass was good stuff for farmers, soldiers, hicks, and thieves; it was too silent for an honest city boy. He had no desire to be a boy scout, he thought comfortably, and fell asleep. He did not dream for the first time in months.

9

The morning was hot and Ike-o became sticky with the heat and anticipation of that evening. He concentrated on his meeting with Dolly; the thought was cooling. He dressed in a fresh uniform, lacing tightly his boots and adjusting his sunglasses. He swaggered out down Mechanic Avenue. The heat of the gray day he felt as intensely as if it were directed solely at him with a personal anger, and, when he came to where he could see Miss Fireman's through the dust, he decided to use her showers.

A cop rousted a man sleeping in a doorway as Ike-o passed. The man explained as he backed away, as best he could with a bloody shin, that his eyes had not been closed ten minutes when the kind officer had rightfully informed him that what he was doing was illegal. His aunt, Mrs. Busby, had given him permission to use her doorway, he said. The numbers writers paid six hundred to one, but Ike-o thought the odds should have been higher for a bum dumb enough to be still asleep in the searchlighted Mechanic Avenue morning.

Inside Miss Fireman's, Ike-o bought soap and rented a towel. From where Ike-o stood, in an alcove between the main building and the glass doors leading out to the playground, he could see the interior of the building and Mechanic Avenue outside. His uneasiness in the familiar building became stronger. It was odd to think that Miss Sarah J. Fireman was not anywhere in this place that carried her imprint everywhere a person looked: on each fought-for sandbox, every potted plant, the refinished desks and chairs, the murals showing the rabbi and the priest, the colored man and the Chinaman, conned from some painter for the price of two seventy-five-cent squares a day at Cohen's. All of the people in the painting had big, beefy faces and little bodies as if the artist was trying to prove that a person could recognize the difference between the slum people if he looked into their oversized faces first. The faces were black, blue, or a white like death, marked off so even an idiot could tell the difference between the struggling lumps in the painting.

"You thinking of collecting art?" he heard and turned from the painting quickly, in his swinging around almost knocking Percy Leech to the ground. "Hey," the little man said, "I came in here for a shower, not the amateur fights."

"I'm home," Ike-o cried again happily. "I beat the rap." The implication was that he had chewed the army up into pieces and spat it out at his leisure. Shaking hands with Leech, he wished it were true.

"Oh, things changed," Leech said, blinking his popped blue-green eyes. "Oh, things ain't what they used to be."

One of the faces from home, intense with its mixture of

deceit and innocence, larceny hovering about every pore where there was no powder. "Leech," Ike-o murmured, almost with disbelief at the realness of the little man, "it's good to see you."

"Leech by name," the grifter used to say, "but tiger by nature. I ain't clawed no one, as I remember today, but don't let my clean fingernails fool you — they been dipped in blood plenty of times." He would hold aloft his soft, infant's hands, shooting back his oversized shirt with its heavy cuff links. "I'm ferocious," he used to say, "don't fall patsy to my good breeding — there ain't nothing I can do about my good manners." He would spit on the floor to show just where good manners could end with him and how quick if the occasion should arise. "I don't have pride," he used to say, and this hardly needed expression as there was never anyone who believed differently. "You can't trade pride up in the butcher shop for sausage, and anything Percy Leech don't need, Percy Leech ain't got time for — don't leech my name in that tone of voice like it gives you something on me."

His name wasn't Leech anyhow but something longer from a Polish past. He looked out, hope nearly busting a blood vessel in his neck, at his gray world with its solid oak doors and avenues drifting to four directions of the compass, and the twisting fire escapes giving him an alternative of moving upward. "Don't leech me, Mother," he used to say, "there ain't nothing you got I want. Unless you're carrying a fiver you don't need. Don't hurt yourself, honey, just let me hold it until the fifth when my check comes."

Who else lived from month to month on prospects of a government disability check that never came for a service in World War I that had never happened? He was no liar — you name it, Leech would do it; he had not the false notions and pride that bound, limited, and hampered lesser men.

"It ain't the same no more, kid," Percy Leech said, "we're all waiting for the garbage collector. We're gone, finished. The Catfish is a bum, so what does that make his barber?"

Percy Leech's bow tie bobbed when he talked. He rattled along like a child's machine gun, tup-tup-tup, and followed his listeners with popped blue-green eyes. He had been told by a fortuneteller his eyes were hypnotic; he stared at people every opportunity he had. He could have hugged Ike-o, he was that pleased someone was happy to see him.

"I bother you?" he asked Ike-o suddenly. "I bore you?"

"No, no," Ike-o said, "no."

"Then why do you look at me as if I was plate glass?" he asked. "Mother, the man's all solid. There ain't nothing to observe on the other side. You got a look on your face like you were going to break into prayer."

Ike-o breathed heavily in the dusty, leaden air. He could see two blocks of Mechanic Avenue through the rear glass doors and chain link fence which surrounded the playground. The curbstone of the street held the usual idle crowd in every posture, leaning, sprawling, jigging, sleeping, standing, running, all of the thousands who had no hopeful future but the day's policy number at four o'clock. He had thought he was different; yet who did he know who jigged more at someone else's command than himself? That was the way the crowds of the world came to congregate, Ike-o decided, wiping with a large army handkerchief the hot back of his neck. The crowds stood around wherever life promised them something better, squatted, marched, and lived according to better times coming. But their faces were not big; a person couldn't tell one from another at fifty yards. Ike-o Hartwell's own face was not oversized except to himself.

"I don't know what's the matter with me," Ike-o said. "Honest to God, it ain't you, Percy. You make me feel good. I feel good looking at you."

"I got that way about me," Leech said. "Some guys I make millionaires, I'm nothing but good luck to them."

They went indoors, Ike-o anticipating the cold shower, but the water was rusty and not fast. It came out tepid, neither hot enough nor cold. Ike-o dried himself, feeling that he had wasted his time. He still sweated; his khaki shirt had huge round dark streaks under his arms and a triangle across his back with a peak at the base of his spine. But Percy Leech had listened to Ike-o's troubles about a suitable tombstone for his father's grave and said the problem was as good as solved. "Why do you still wear that long face?" Leech asked. "Ain't I solved your problem?"

Ike-o had not told him of his love for Dolly — no one in Sobaski's Stairway would have given him six to five on that — or his pain at being thrown out of the army like a stray cat. "I guess you're right, Leech," Ike-o said. "I ain't got nothing wrong with me."

"That's the boy," Leech said.

On the sidewalk before Sladic's Memorials, YOU ONLY GET WHAT YOU PAY FOR, Ike-o saw the exact marker for Charlie Hartwell. He walked around the giant statue, noting the profound quiet on the white marble face, the sunlight falling gently on the combed head of Jesus Christ. He touched the cool stone reverently and wiped off dust from the pedestal on which the statue stood.

"This got to be it," Ike-o said, feeling excited about the rightness of the ten-foot height, the shining white stone. "What's the angle, Percy? — You ever see a statue like that in your life?"

The little man blinked his hypnotic eyes. "Never," he said, "I never did. He looks like he's going to come down off that block and shake hands with me. Look at that hand stretched out to give a sinner five." He pulled Ike-o along down Eleventh Street, pushing him as Ike-o stopped to look back. "Keep walking," Percy said, from the side of his mouth, "don't let on, kid, keep walking."

In a corner numbers joint at Eleventh and Pacific, Percy persuaded Ike-o that only a chump would pay out the money for a beautiful statue like that one. Now, Spook Novakovitch's cousin Sam had a three-quarter-ton truck that could be made available that week. And with the two of them, Sam, maybe the Catfish, and another guy, they could simply heist the statue one night about midnight, with only a fee for a truck rental and twenty bucks for the strange accomplice. Ike-o was dubious, laughing some times but shaking his head so seriously at every moment that Percy Leech stopped to catch his breath, but Percy was positive about his talents. "I should have been a master criminal," he said. "I got all the right instincts."

Soda-pop cases were piled like stalagmites in a dusty cave in Cohen's back room. When O. C. Gedunsky heard the plan he laughed, sitting up on the Ten Strike Bowling Machine, where he had been taking his late morning nap. He stepped into his shoes, blowing dust from the back room from the patent leather, still laughing to himself. He tied his shoes sitting on the low metal railing of the bowling machine. "Don't bump one of them stacks of pop cases," he said, "or we'll be under a ton of wood." He shook hands with Ike-o, holding both of Ike-o's hands with his two hands. "I thought you had good sense, Isaac," he said. "You and the tiger would get twenty years for bad judgment alone. The nerve! — going down there to Eleventh Street to snatch a statue. Novakovitch's cousin Sam ain't been seen in Sobaski's Stairway for four months — I hear he violated his parole. And, you, Mr. Dillinger, where do you know anyone can carry his own weight, not to say a five-pound bag of sugar? I thought you had good sense, Isaac."

"Give us another idea that good," Leech said.

"Pay for the statue," Gedunsky said, "you ever think of that? Buy the statue, take it on time, pay for it. You ever bought anything, Leech?"

"There ain't no reason for you to know my business," Leech said. "What's it your business if I ever bought anything? — I bought my mother a sewing machine once."

Gedunsky hooted. "I remember," he howled. "God rest her soul, you stole your mother's Singer sewing machine and I gave you the money to get it back out of the pawnshop. That's right, tiger — you did kind of buy it."

"I don't remember the details," Leech said, "but you always did have a good memory, Catfish. I'll take your word."

"Thanks," Gedunsky said, bending his knees to peer into the rear glass panel of the bowling machine. He combed his wavy white hair by the reflection against the girl with fancy tights and ten crudely drawn flying bowling pins.

The three men sat at the counter in Cohen's, blowing their coffee cool, wild talk rattling around their heads: nothing secret about counter talk in Cohen's, but conversation shouted and outshouted, conned, contrived, every third word some kind of lie, want, or wish.

"I'm getting married," Ike-o said, an air of finality as abrupt as a confession in his quick turn to see the Catfish's reaction.

"You asked the party yet?" Gedunsky asked. He slid around on his stool and stood. Leech stood with him. "I can't hear myself think," the Catfish said. "Come outside." He put his hand on Percy Leech's thin chest as he too started for the door. "Stay here," the Catfish said, "I'm expecting a call."

"Who from," Leech asked, sitting again, "the morgue? Who else needs you?"

Rain fell down the Catfish's face, seeping around the juts and crags to find his white shirt and black suit coat. "Who, may I ask, is the lucky girl?"

"You know damned well who. Come off it, Oscar."

"Well, well," Gedunsky said. "Ain't that going to be the

happy marriage?" The daylight neon reflected like trickery in his eyes; the green Cohen's sign twinkled in the hollows of Gedunsky's face.

"That's one fine family," O. C. Gedunsky said, mockery not yet taking its final twist. Ike-o listened sadly and with a growing anger. "I hear one of the sisters in that fine family is getting married," Gedunsky said, almost shyly. "Rita, by name, I hear Rita Smolcher is getting married. I stayed up all one night imagining all the celebrities who were going to be there. Thaddeus Smolcher himself, he'll be there, maybe with one of the high yellows from Mother Ida's and his sons, maybe handcuffed together for law and order and a few of the sisters organizing some free-lance action in the men's john. I been ruminating about that wedding — ain't it nice you gave me another fine wedding to think about?"

"You are a buzzard," Ike-o said.

"I'm the best friend you got," the Catfish said, before he strode away in the rain. "Everything's changed, Isaac," he said, "you been gone three years. People change."

Ike-o caught him by the arm, swinging the Catfish until he looked directly into his haunted face. "Make good," Ike-o cried. "What do you know about Dolly Smolcher, Catfish? I mean her personally. Don't give me an account of the family tree."

"I thought you had sense," the Catfish said, not looking at Ike-o or answering his question either. The Catfish held his peace. "I'm getting wet, Isaac," he said, walking away slowly up Mechanic Avenue. "Rain is bad for my sinuses. Go pay for the coffee, I got business in the Police Station."

"There ain't nothing changed," Ike-o called, watching him go with a mounting fury that flesh and blood could not fly at words, especially the words of Gedunsky which were never quite uttered. "You're the same fourflusher you always were," Ike-o confided at the top of his lungs to Sobaski's Stairway. "You're lousy — you stink, Gedunsky." Ike-o brushed away rain water from his face. "I'm fifty times the man you are," he called. "Your name is mud with me. Go ahead, Gedunsky, crawl into the woodwork with the other roaches. You ever mention a certain party's name I'll break your jaw." He shouted it loud enough for it to reach Gedunsky a block up Mechanic Avenue.

"Remember," Gedunsky called back, "I'm the best friend you got, punk."

Tiny pinpricks of rain fell in the bars of neon-reflected light on the pavement. The afternoon was dark. Ike-o swaggered toward Sladic's on Eleventh Street; he walked like a soldier. "I'm worth a dozen of him!" he muttered. "And so is Dolly!" In half a block the deception had worn away, leaving him not angry but tired, a dumb brute whom nobody had told the score or even the name of the game.

Then Ike-o slowed down his bold, paratrooper's walk; he shuffled along with his head down, natty uniform, boots, and all. The bright place of his youth had been Mechanic Avenue. But the light had been in his youth and his father, and happiness had been as temporary as the neon moons of the long street, vanishing when love and youth had gone. The light was absent for good from his imagination. Ike-o felt now that the shadows no longer stopped at Mechanic

Avenue. It was Ike-o Hartwell, the phony paratrooper, who brought them with him wherever he walked. The green, red, and white curlicued neon lights of Mechanic Avenue knew him too well to be fooled by his bold soldier's swagger. He could raise a holler at Gedunsky, curse the lights, but wherever he put down his boot there was darkness spreading out like pools of water underfoot. "How do you do?" he asked of his reflection in the window of Professor Chandu's Health Store. It was not a happy re-introduction. There were not one but two men in the window glass: a soldier with a blurry drunk draped around his neck. The drunk crept in with the shadows, the same drunk who had been the sunshine of the little boy's imagination. Now he staggered along with Ike-o the man, hugging him closely, so near that a stranger would have thought them one man, but Ike-o knew the limits of the dark drunkard. He held fast as long as there was a debt to be paid him — then like any pawnbroker he would disappear behind the three-dollar overcoat rack into the blackness of his private vaults. There had to be a real sun somewhere; the paratrooper was not phony, he was the real, brave Ike-o Hartwell. Sing for boldness, sing for bravery. "I can't give you anything but love, baby," Ike-o sang into the approaching Mechanic Avenue dusk. Dolly had waited for him, what else mattered?

The blood itself sang in the brave Ike-o Hartwell. He would work his fingers down to bone to put the drunkard on his shoulder to bed forever. What shadow was that which dared lay on his path toward Eleventh Street and Sladic's Memorials? Ike-o leaped a fireplug, still singing.

He made his deal with the younger Sladic, fifty dollars a month for ten months; it was big money for a marker, but Ike-o's charity was great too. "Put it in the back now," he said, "I don't want nobody lighting matches on my old man's statue." Sladic assured him the statue was safe.

There was a full bright moon, but the night was dark in the shadow of Emma Carnavan's bus where Ike-o paced. He circled the bus and listened. A radio played inside and he heard the kids and Emma Carnavan singing along with the radio music. Dolly wasn't there yet. He finally stood quietly in a shadow of the bus; he did not want to attract the roving, desperate bums who lived out past Fifteenth Street.

She came toward the silvery clearing with another person, her sister Rita. He heard their feet grinding the bright specks of glass before he saw them. She was not dressed as a man. Her blonde hair was long put piled bravely and golden on her head. It shone white in the moonlight. The same high, pale forehead, blue eyes even in shadow, the same straight legs and graceful walk. She was a full head taller than her sister. With a sound of crunched glass, he stepped out into the speckled clearing. He forgot his prepared speech.

"I'll bet you never thought you'd see me here," he said.

They were startled but recognized him immediately. He took Dolly's white hand to shake it and did not release it. "You're not going to win any prizes for letter writing," he said.

"It wasn't because I wasn't thinking of you," Dolly said.

Years piled up carelessly like Emma's cordwood around the bus, waiting for winter and her stove, stacked, lonely, long; the years no longer existed between Ike-o and Dolly. He stood in the moonlight holding her hand, not conscious of Rita. He felt once again the clear-brained Ike-o Hartwell, the passionate, honest boy. Standing there at arm's length she was again as in one of his C-9 dreams, his pale kid beauty of Sobaski's Stairway.

"I missed you something terrible," Ike-o said. "I have a lot to tell you."

He did not notice the sudden turn away, the small cough at things to be told, matters to be cleared up before they truly could stand again innocently and with love in the moonlight. He saw only the gentle little girl, the quiet one who paid for the frantic adventures of the other Smolchers with a silent pain. He saw only that deep in her eyes was the same hurt clouding the blue.

She had not forgotten him.

"There wasn't a day passed I didn't think of you," she said.

And still they stood, not awkwardly but at arm's length, her arm slim and white and a beautiful length in the moonlight.

"I know what you mean," Ike-o said.

She had hoped he would appear somehow just like this, step from a shadow somewhere into white moonlight and take her and fly with her, as he had promised, a million miles from Sobaski's Stairway. Dolly smiled, her teeth bright by the white moon, and held his hand tightly.

"We've got lots of news too," Rita said. "Old man-hater

herself is going to get married." It was a family fiction among the Smolcher girls that the reason for the dearth of husbands in the clan lay somehow within them; they were manless, the family myth went, because they wanted to be.

"Yeah," Ike-o said, embarrassed, "that's a surprise, ain't it? Never thought a man could talk you into anything."

"Well, he ain't much," Rita said with a small laugh, "but he's a man and he suits me fine. George Grinnek, the veteran."

Grinnie the Gimp, the old street soldier, maybe thirty-two, maybe fifty-two, a veteran of the campaigns on Mechanic Avenue with his coat collar turned up in the winter and in an undershirt in the summer, he still lived and waited to be Rita's hapless groom.

"He got a good job running an elevator now," Rita said. "Steady."

"That's swell," Ike-o said, "that's swell, he's a lucky guy."

Grinnie used to bum nickels for wine from the school kids in Miller School. He walked with a limp acquired in a bar so far back in a confused past it was not even a clear memory, the place or the quarrel or who did it, who picked him up and threw him down a flight of stairs in the back. "I asked this French fellow where was the john, not too good, not knowing the language," Grinnie always said, "and he sure showed me the hard way," claiming the catastrophe had happened in France; but there had not passed twenty minutes in his lifetime when George Grinnek wasn't within mothering distance of Sobaski's Stairway.

"He's gassed from the first war," Rita said, "but he's got very many good qualities."

"Yeah," Ike-o said.

"He don't hardly drink any more," Rita said. "He's real steady."

"Don't tell us any more about him," Dolly said. "He is what he is."

"No," Rita said, pushing out aimlessly, "there's a lot people don't know about him, not being close up — he got a heart of gold. Georgie. He could buy the Gulf Building if everyone owed him money was to pay him back at once."

They stood silently.

"Well, am I lying?" Rita asked. "Do you know any different?"

"I guess not," Dolly said.

"Look, honey," Ike-o said to Dolly, not pulling her close but releasing her hand and walking three feet away, and turning his back to her as if there would be a greater intimacy in allowing her to hear words he said into the night rather than directly to her while he held her close. "Look, Dolly, I asked you to marry me a long time ago and you said yes and it was all agreed and in every letter we both said it was going to be just that way. And a lot of things could have happened between then and now and you might have changed your mind fifty times over and I ain't holding you to any foolish thing you said when we were kids, or maybe not such kids, but I ain't holding you anyhow. I only want to say I'm holding myself to what I asked because there ain't a thing in my mind different — like I walked down to the corner for a pack of cigarettes and come back ten minutes later."

He searched the ground and spoke to it, daring only there to plant words that he had never known he could say. "I love you in the same way as when we were kids," he said, not caring that Rita heard. "I always will. There ain't no other direction where I care to go but you, Dolly. You say the right thing, honey, and there'll be two marriages in your family soon. It scares me, Dolly, I love you so much."

She came and placed both her hands on his khaki shoulders and Ike-o turned and kissed Dolly. She slid her arms around his neck and he pulled her close. There was no wind on the dark night; the broken glass glittered by the moon and the silent brown loam of Sobaski's Stairway did not stir with grass. A train passed far away, breathing hard, and a streetcar clanged on the tracks down on Mechanic Avenue. Ike-o heard the streetcar finally. The night had sounds and movement somewhere beyond them after all. Ike-o released Dolly gently.

"I've got things to do," Rita said.

But before they could separate they were stopped by the sounds of someone approaching; they stood like transfixed rabbits, hoping that the new arrival would not be dangerous to them. The thicket thundered with familiar, lumbering Fats Smolcher crashing like another species of wood beast along the lonely path in the woods. He paused to observe them from above the incline of his paunch, folding his arms over his great stomach as if he would conceal the wine bottle which protruded from his shirt.

"I heard you was back," he said. "Ain't it nice to see you, Isaac." He seemed to sniff the night air with his head tilted back for clues to what was what between Dolly and Ike-o. He waited.

"They're going to get married," Rita said.

"That tickles me," Fats said, "this is a momentous occasion."

He took the bottle out from his shirt with a broad flourish, whipped off the cork, took a great pull, and passed the wine around. "Well, ain't that the good news," he said.

"I don't think I've ever been happier," Ike-o said, drinking from Fats' bottle. Dolly complained that she was not dressed for the occasion and that the kids inside the bus still needed to be bathed. "Except for it being the happiest night of my life too," she said, "it's the worst night in two and one-half years for seeing you again. I took home some papers three weeks ago for my boss and I haven't typed them yet. He has to have them tomorrow." They agreed he would see her again the following night at the same place; she watched him carefully, waiting for a sign that he had heard anything about her.

She believed she loved him, yet she wanted time to think, to see the thing from his point of view. She had agreed to marry him and had no regrets. What had she to lose? She had no reservations. They held each other for a long time when he kissed her again. Then he left the clearing near the bus, hoping to find a friend who would drink at least a beer with him on the momentous good news.

A Checker taxicab pulled up to Ike-o as he walked down Mechanic Avenue, and the driver leaned toward the window and said, "Hop in, general, it's on the house." Ike-o shook hands with the driver, a curly blond, excitable neighborhood man named Buddy Mogus. "Where to, kid? — it's on me," Mogus said.

"I'll tell you first," Ike-o said. "I'm getting married."

"Yeah," Mogus said. "A girl you met in the service? — local girl?" Buddy Mogus was a few years older than Ike-o, but like most cab drivers he thought he was a traveling encyclopedia of city-wide information. He liked news too much for Ike-o to answer quickly. "Dolly Smolcher," Ike-o said, after a few moments.

Mogus said nothing, cruising slowly two blocks, and then he said, "That's a hell of a family you're getting mixed up with, kid."

"Look, hackie," Ike-o said, "is there something you know that I don't about Dolly Smolcher?"

Mogus pulled the cab up to the curb. "I ain't out looking for an argument," he said.

"Okay," Ike-o said, "okay, thanks for the ride." He stepped out again on the pavement of Mechanic Avenue and then turned back. "Remember, I got the Catfish to testify for you that time you were in trouble in that case of mistaken identity. I thought we were friends. Why don't you wise me up?"

Mogus said, "I want to stay friends." He stopped to think. "I got a proposition for you, I need a partner."

"I still ain't wise," Ike-o said.

"Let me ask you one question, Ike-o: Do you think the cops would ever look for a guy who stuck up service stations and left by taxi? Huh? — do you think?"

Ike-o laughed, relieved that he had forgotten the one-track, cab-driving mentalities of Mechanic Avenue for the moment — they always fished up angles, finding them even in situations like Dolly's where there was only an accident family. "I told you, hackie, I'm getting married," Ike-o said. "If I was the best stick-up man in town I'd quit right now. Which I ain't and don't want to be."

Mogus smacked himself on the forehead. "I'd like you to drive this cab for one month, just one month, then see if you'd laugh in my face when I offer you something good. Every strong-arm man comes to town hires my cab and hits me in the head — shoes, blackjacks, flashlights, anything on my head."

"What about the drunks you roll?" Ike-o asked.

Mogus put his cab in gear. "What are you, a detective? — you're too dumb to know a good thing."

"Shove off, small time," Ike-o said. "Make one wrong remark and I'll punch you in the head. With my fist."

"You ain't so smart, Isaac."

"You ever think of buying a thing and paying for it?" Ike-o asked. "You're a crook and a punk, get lost."

"Oh, you're one wise guy," Mogus said, and drove away, leaving Ike-o to stand alone on Mechanic Avenue. He bought six bottles of beer and took them home with him, not wishing, on what should be a happy night, to be immersed again in Sobaski's Stairway's constant high tide of suspicion.

10

The buildings Dolly and Ike-o passed had small wooden steps at the heavy front doors where people had once sat and talked and called out to each other from house to house and across the cobbled street. "I remember when you couldn't walk down this street," Ike-o said, "for all the people crowding the sidewalk."

"Me, too," Dolly said. "I remember."

The street was empty, and the wind blew along gray curbs. In the upper windows the moon made faces in the window glass and fell on the walls of the buildings on the opposite side of the street as strongly and as boldly black as sunlight.

"This is no place for a girl to live alone," Ike-o said.

"It's not bad," Dolly said. "I always have Rita with me."

The children they carried were both asleep; Ike-o held the girl closely to him so that her head would not bob. He heard her breathing and felt the warm breath against his neck. "Kids can sleep anywhere, can't they?" Ike-o asked.

"I wish I were a kid," Dolly said.

They walked slowly and stately, balancing the children on their shoulders. "I'd move away from here in a minute," Dolly said, "if it wasn't that I wanted to watch these kids. Being a kid should be the best time of life."

"Not for me it wasn't. I'd like to punch somebody in the face when I think of all the lies told to kids."

They stopped before a building like all the rest, flat, windowed, gray and brown and dirty. "When they tearing this dump down?" Ike-o asked.

"A month," Dolly said, "two months. I got my eviction notice two weeks ago."

Their footsteps fell hollow in the old building. It was not as large as the apartment houses on Gardenia Street but divided into only one three-room apartment on each floor. There were three floors, but the first floor was vacant; their footsteps sounded of themselves and a larger echo as they walked up the narrow hallway.

Dolly put the children into one room and came out to where Ike-o sat on a couch in the living room. She lit a cigarette.

"I smoke now," she said.

"I see," Ike-o said.

He stretched his feet with their boots out before him. These rooms were like every room in Sobaski's Stairway, somehow; they gave off old sweat and the smell of dried wallpaper, and their color was dirty. But he had never been in a room alone with Dolly before — wasn't that something? — two street people alone in a room after knowing each other all these years. And the room was made different by her. She brought a cleanness to it; it would take more than a dingy room to take away from that swift, straight blonde girl with eyes blue and legs white and arms long and capable. She had handled the children like a juggler, passing them from hand to hand and into pajamas and into bed without waking them.

She came and sat on the couch near him.

"You make me nervous," he said, standing and walking away from her.

The living room's one window opened on a courtyard where two different houses put their garbage. Ike-o stood looking out at a blank wall, but at the top there cut across the roof and a triangle of the wall a silver splash of moonlight. He stood undecided with his back to Dolly, looking at the blank wall.

"I want you so bad," Ike-o said, "I ain't responsible. I ain't going to treat you like just another dame."

She stood and watched him. "It couldn't be like that with you and me," she said. "You said yourself a long time ago that Ike-o and Dolly were different, that there weren't anything but good things going to happen to us as long as we had each other."

He turned and looked at her and loved her but did not move.

"You were what kept me going," he said. "I shouldn't tell you — you'll get a big head if you knew how much you were in my mind."

"Mine too," she said, "mine too, does that make it even?"

He held her close and kissed her and, still holding her, he slid her toward the couch and sat and leaned her backward and buried his face into her hot neck. He took her long hair into his hand and pulled her close.

"No, Ike-o," she said and stood.

She sat on the edge of the room's one bed. "Come here," she said, "and sit down." She patted the bed. "Come on," she said, "come sit here."

He sat on the bed with her. "You ain't afraid?" he asked.

"I love you," she said, "and it had to be on a bed."

He kissed her again, and again pushed her backward. He unbuttoned her dress but did not touch her directly. "You're not afraid?" he asked, unable to breathe evenly.

"I love you," she said, "I always have and I always will."

Her dress was unbuttoned; she lay back with her long blonde thighs mocking him. Still he did not move toward her. He held her face in his hands, shutting out everything but the innocence in the eyes.

"This is the way it's always going to be with us," he said.

She kissed him and held him close.

"Never anything but truth between us," he said.

Her eyes became misty. "We're not the same," Dolly said, sitting up. "Don't touch me, Ike-o, until you hear what I say."

Ike-o sat up, listening to her, but fascinated by her open dress and the white undergarments he saw. He clenched his fist; he did not like this — they should not have stopped.

"That boy in there, that baby," she said, "Richard, that's not a kid my mother abandoned. That's my kid, that's my son."

Ike-o sat still, waiting.

"I did a bad thing when you were gone, Ike-o," she said, "but I can't leave the baby. I was mixed-up and lonely and so in love with you I hadn't anywhere else to turn and I did some dumb things."

"Wouldn't the guy marry you?"

"I love you, Ike-o. What do I care about that guy?"

Sobaski's Stairway rumors stood with Ike-o Hartwell. They flanked him and whispered insinuations, while he tried to think. There were many men, not one; and once she was married who could ever trust her again, because if she did the wrong thing once she'd do it again and again. Midnight logic, of men and weak women and especially the Smolcher girls and Sobaski's Stairway dirt and hopelessness. And how many men knew things about the blonde girl he did not?

Dolly stood and turned and buttoned her dress.

"Get that look off your face," she said.

An army of dark questions surrounded him. Ike-o stood helplessly listening and unable to answer. A girl who had a baby out of wedlock was a no-good whore, and there wasn't anywhere else a man could look for an answer except into that irrefutable logic of what other men had said.

"Well, say something," she said, still not turning.

Ike-o left her standing there on the threadbare rug in the grimy, flower-walled apartment, walking out into the hallway and down the echoing stairs. Women were all the same; he should have known, he thought.

"Ike-o!"

He heard her voice in the dark hall corridor but did not

turn back. The moon skipped from window to window of the third floor, but Ike-o did not see. He cried softly, thinking that at least Dolly was honest enough to give him the facts. But hadn't she known he would find out? The Catfish had known and so had everybody else on Mechanic Avenue. Her honesty was another trick to entangle him. Putting her in her place, walking out on her, and treating her like the whore she was, did him no good. He still cried for the hurt that she had done to him.

11

Ike-o took work with a salvage company owned by a man named Con Purbanko. Ike-o worked with a construction gang in Sobaski's Stairway, tearing up streetcar tracks and plumbing, working on the ground he remembered from his childhood. And each day, under his boots and heavy matted gloves, there was less to Sobaski's Stairway. Over behind Miss Fireman's building, up on Pig Alley, there lingered still a few battered old walls, the last of a Bible institute. Ike-o's crew worked there in July. The Bible institute's walls crouched on the street above Mechanic Avenue like a memory of gray guilt: jagged old bricks, scarred doors, a spider's predatory framework of humped-back concrete walls. Faded and dedicated and now vanished missionaries to Sobaski's Stairway, as unremembered as the sinners whose souls they had contested for with Mechanic Avenue, had once encamped there. But they had been forced by the state redevelopment commission to drift away like mortar dust in a strong wind to seek other sinners. That was their only option; otherwise they would have been compelled to rehabilitate each other. In memoriam, their wooden flooring had been torn out by local sinners on Pig Alley still needing heat. Their windows now hung shattered and disembodied and lonesome for the armies of hopheads, darbs, and alcoholics who no longer washed them at fifty cents a day on the ugly quicksand road to rehabilitation. Pig Alley was gone too, a shanty row of women's heads poking through doorways and plastic-curtained windows while the Mississippi girls inside, stood on mud floors and humped on corn pallets for a quarter a trick.

Conrad Purbanko hovered daily in the sunlight over his cigar, hardly ever moving his lips to speak, and then only to say, "Step it up, jack, get it going." A big man with broad beefy shoulders in a rolled-sleeve white shirt, and a hulking, angry nose, he seemed concentrated in all of his furious and destructive nature down to the glowing brown tube in his mouth. He was a professional wrecker, a destroyer of buildings throughout the United States. He puffed his cigar only long enough to retain life there. He wasted no motion, not even a breath, as if he would not give the world one thing more than necessity compelled him. He received no enjoyment from the smoke. He received little enjoyment from anything except the sound and sight of things rent and of annihilation. If the cigar were the world, he could not have assailed it more violently between his antediluvian jaws. He frowned all day and into the night. He seemed to have come from nowhere, but to have been created in one piece, in one moment, an arrogant giant in a straw hat among the rubble of Mechanic Avenue. He said he had once lived in Sobaski's Stairway, but no one remembered him.

In due course the demolition companies working their way up Mechanic Avenue attacked the Sarah J. Fireman Center. Her prized tile floor was lifted and shipped somewhere. The coveted slides and swings were packed away in wooden boxes and sent to other charities. The wondering scrutiny of Miss Fireman's watery old eyes did not halt the demolition. Occasionally she was too ill to leave her hotel room in Oakland to be there at the site, but she came on other days, leaning on a cane.

A warm whirlpool wind came up in the afternoons, nestling down hot and greedy on the cranes and half walls; the wind lodged a fine red dust along the length of what had been Mechanic Avenue. A red dust carpet was made for all the wooden steps leading from the vanished tenants' cellars to nowhere. Miss Fireman coughed on the dust, and one summer afternoon did an odd thing. She shuffled out to where nothing stood but a tilted, hastily thrown-together shack with a water pipe in it. The demolition laborers had come to stand there for a few minutes every day. There, shielded from the sun and dust, they drank cold water from the pipe.

Miss Fireman asked Purbanko to leave the shack standing. He looked at her curiously; possibly he thought, even while he nodded his head and agreed, that there might be a time in the future when the shack would have some value, some meaning, and of the greater pleasure that would be his when he destroyed it then. "Well, you can have it," he said, implicit in his agreement the understanding that it was hers until he came with his power of destruction to remove it.

The next day Miss Fireman came back. She dragged from a taxicab a painting of Van Gogh, head wrapped with a bandage; two folding chairs, one for her and the other for humanity; and a strong Samson card table. She set up the chairs and table and nailed the picture to the wall. She sat at one of the chairs, almost smiling, not outside on the low wooden fence looking in, near tears, observing the world from her rightful place.

That summer, while a false dawn stained the uneasy sky over Sobaski's Stairway, Ike-o dressed quickly in his army fatigues before his mother awoke. He put on a baseball cap and his paratrooper boots.

He used a shovel and an eighteen-pound steel bar for digging, hacking away at the spent, disinherited brown earth of Sobaski's Stairway as if the ground had harmed him or was the cause of his misery. In the long afternoons, when the foreman was not observing, he squatted in the shade of a crane or truck and ate meatball sandwiches and drank cold water from a Thermos jug. Counting over the money he had saved, adding sums for each week he would work, his mind feverishly threading through figures and his ambition to put the statue over his father's grave, still it was good to feel in his mouth the juices of food and cold water on his dry throat.

Con Purbanko found him sitting on the fender of the truck one afternoon. Ike-o stood and wiped his hands on his fatigues and waited. Purbanko put his heavy hand on Ike-o's shoulder, not angry but firm.

"You going to marry that little Polish girl?"

"What little Polish girl is that?"

"Fats Smolcher's daughter."

"What gave you that idea?" Ike-o asked.

Purbanko released his hold and turned to look with his heavy, opaque eyes at Ike-o. "Her father told me," he said.

"That's his opinion," Ike-o said.

"Okay."

Ike-o moved away a few feet. "What business is it of yours?"

"I don't like you," Purbanko said. "There ain't nothing I like about you. Go collect your pay five o'clock."

"I can go now," Ike-o said.

"Five o'clock," Purbanko said, turning and walking away, adjusting his straw hat against the sun.

Ike-o Hartwell despised himself for being so weak as to let a tramp daughter of Fats Smolcher's enter his thoughts, twist the thoughts around until she was the day and the heat and the hard rock, the cruel bar, and the far-off merciless sun. She would not let him dig in peace — what if Conrad Purbanko had eyes for her? — she was game for any man who had the inclination. The bar bit into the rock, gouged at it. There was a way to turn the bar exactly as it struck the ground to best loosen the earth. Ike-o worked savagely, not caring that it was his last afternoon. Dolly was finished business, he thought; she was just another Sobaski's Stairway floozie whom he owed nothing, not even thought. Ike-o's sweat ran down his forehead into his eyes. He was nearly halfway home to his unpaid debt to his mother. He had saved two hundred dollars toward his father's statue. He owed two hundred more, having already given Sladic a hundred dollars.

That night Ike-o brought his mother black bread from Fischer's Bakery; it was a favorite of hers and rumbled in her stomach long hours after it was consumed. She sliced the bread directly into triangles and smeared one section with mayonnaise. She delicately licked the mayonnaise from her bread knife. Her tongue was small for such a huge round face.

"You got to stop watching that television set so much," Ike-o said. She was paying Low Man Luster, the door-to-door peddler, a dollar a week for it. "You're going to ruin your eyesight altogether watching it all day that way."

"If you'd listen to me," she said, excited, "we wouldn't have to be sitting here while Charlie lays out in the hot sun. You wouldn't be digging ditches you listen to me."

"Ah, Ma," Ike-o said.

"The two of us could go on *Strike It Rich*," she said. "There's people like us on it every day. All we do is tell our story and I'll bet everybody in the place will be crying for your poor daddy."

Ike-o left the apartment. "Why don't you sit by the window any more?" he asked. "That television set is going to drive you crazy."

There was no one down on Gardenia Street whose career Yolanda followed. The hucksters with their horses and wagons no longer came to sell their fruits and vegetables. There was only an occasional fight, but not a good Polish battle with maybe two women locked in each other's hair and swirling into doorways and around cars.

She sat transfixed two feet away from her television set; her eyesight was dim — the figures were only shadows — but she became aware of one man who drifted into the picture and out again no matter the program. "I seen Charlie," she told Ike-o the first time she was positive.

"He was standing with a bunch of people waiting for a train. You remember how he was? Always a little bit off to one side of everybody. Well, there he was, standing there the same as always. When he knew I was looking he waved his hand up at me yoo hoo; I guess he had some thing to drink and he was feeling pretty good."

She saw him repeatedly after that. When he was angry he argued with her and made threatening gestures; sometimes in a festive mood he waved to her to join him. Several times she snapped off the television, falling back into a chair, breathing hard. "Ike-o," she cried. "He's coming after me. He started for me with his balled-up fist."

Sometimes days passed that summer with no sign of Charlie. Yolanda would chuckle appreciatively then. "He got himself off on a tear somewhere," she said, happy at Charlie's ability to do things his way. But he always returned, lurching drunkenly across the screen or appearing miraculously as a face blotting out the rest of the picture, mouthing oaths, and then disappearing when she called Ike-o to see him.

Ike-o wanted her to come with him to a doctor to examine her eyes. "See this," she said, holding aloft her mayonnaise knife, "that's for cutting bread or smearing, it ain't for slicing people." She refused to see a doctor about the cataracts on her eyes. "I see what I see, there ain't nothing wrong with my eyes." It was more logical to her that Charlie Hartwell haunted her than to believe her eyes were bad.

Ike-o would find her late at night sitting before the television set waiting for Charlie to appear.

"Jesus understands," Yolanda screamed one night and would not be quieted. She held Ike-o's hand tightly. "Jesus sees into people's hearts," she said. "He understands when nobody else does." She lay shivering and trembling through her great bulk the long night. Ike-o sat at his radio and listened to dance music.

In the mornings Ike-o bought a newspaper, checked off possible places where he might work, and either called or went directly to be interviewed. It was wasted time. He was happy when in the afternoons he could come back to Sobaski's Stairway to sit with Miss Fireman in her shack. He saw all the goodness in the crumbling ruin that was Sobaski's Stairway in the slight tremble of her old white head. She had no other visitors. Ike-o joined the invisible crowds who still stood at her elbow, murky, faceless, still demanding. She wiped at her dry old lips with a balled tiny handkerchief and repeatedly asked Ike-o what she could do for him. "Nothing," he would say, torn and confused, "everything's just fine with me."

12

Mr. Thaddeus Smolcher hired a hall and invited everyone he knew to the wedding reception of his daughter Rita and her new groom George Grinnek. Whoever in Sobaski's Stairway had nowhere else to go that Saturday night, with the exception of a sullen Ike-o Hartwell, made preparations to attend the festivities at Souick's Social Hall. Mechanic Avenue blossomed anew by twilight. The Catfish wore a white carnation and had one for Percy Leech and Three-belly Kelski; earlier that day, while the bride and groom were out riding and blasting the horn in a Buick of a cousin of Grinnek's from Morgantown, West Virginia, Fats had bought out a flower store of carnations, and, drunk and unable to function further, had dragged the carnations in a huge carton into Cohen's and gasped to the Catfish, "See all my friends get one." That had been at two o'clock, and it was presumed by the men who walked around Fats sprawled in a back booth in Cohen's, one large black polished shoe blocking the aisle, that their host would recover in plenty of time to greet them that night at Souick's Social Hall.

Fats' head felt as if a plaster cast sat directly on the crown, but he was not sad. He tingled with joy when he reminded himself that Rita, old alley cat, was at long last happily married: for eight hours now by the clock over Cohen's gray steam cabinets. That left him only a father's responsibility for Irene and Dolly; he had dismissed from his mind with their mother the disloyal daughters Bertha and Dorothey. They had deserted him simultaneously with Marg, not exactly in concert but singly by bus and on foot, like rats leaving a sinking ship.

"They left me like rats jumping a sinking ship, one at a time," Fats said to Cohen's one-legged counter man, "but there was more to the old battleship any of them knew — there's plenty of life yet in the old rowboat. Teddy Smolcher takes care of his own."

The absence of Ike-o Hartwell from the ceremony that morning in Saint Stephen's worried him as an uncompleted piece of business. He had no doubt that he could marry off Dolly, even with her bad luck, but Fats Smolcher was a neat man mentally. He liked everything in its place in his huge buffalo's mind. If Ike-o Hartwell was up to tricks, God knew there was probably plenty floating around in his blood left over from his old man, then Teddy Smolcher would exert some pressure of his own. Dolly had looked like a princess that morning, like a dream of goodness that afternoon sitting in the Buick and waving good-by at him, and his only unhappiness had been at the absence of the young Protestant. "Coffee," Fats roared. "For the love of

Jesus, set me up black coffee." He looked like a determined man who had an apartment house or a horse or at least two daughters to trade off as he sat gulping the scalding coffee. "Coffee," he shouted for another cup. "I need black coffee, Jasper."

He paraded up Mechanic Avenue to Gardenia Street, happy his feet were themselves again, direct, righteous, and responsive, and, at the corner, he turned to march on the house of Ike-o Hartwell.

He caught Ike-o Hartwell leaving. The boy was dressed to kill in a white shirt and tie. Fats, subtly, ingeniously controlled his anger. He would have punched Ike-o a good one, said, "Now, you son of a bitch, let's get going over to Souick's," but no, craftily he bade his time, not speaking, but blocking the boy's passage up Gardenia. "What's the matter with you?" Ike-o asked.

"Why, good evening, Isaac," Fats said. "I come down to make sure you and your dear mamma was okay. I sent you an invite two weeks ago about Rita being married to-day but I guess since you had to work you couldn't make the ceremony over at Saint Stephen's this morning. I was hoping someone would bring your ma — it being the last wedding reception in Souick's Social Hall, Iggy Souick himself told me — I thought for sure your dear ma and you would be there."

"I was going downtown," Ike-o said, looking away.

"Oh, you forgot the day," Fats said, still a good distance from punching the Protestant to the ground and kicking him a good one for extra measure.

"It's off between Dolly and me," Ike-o said, and took a deep breath.

"Well, heh, heh," Fats giggled, "it ain't off between you and me, is it, Isaac? Or your ma and me? Or your ma and you and the whole world? Why, there's people hate my guts will be drinking my whiskey a half hour from now, and do you think I care? — why, not one cent. If you and Dolly had your little quarrel that ain't the end of the world, is it? Engaged people fight all the time. Don't skip coming for your ma's sake, for me, for Rita and Georgie Grinnek. Why, Christ, 'Where's Ike-o Hartwell,' Georgie asked me this morning. It ain't off between you and everything is it, Isaac?"

"It's pretty final," Ike-o said.

Fats put his arm on Ike-o's shoulder. "I ain't a young man," he said, pulling Ike-o close, "and there ain't much that life could have gave me that I didn't get. But there's one thing missing — a son, you know what I mean, kid? My own boys went wrong somewhere, Isaac — and I always looked on you like a son. Now, I ain't asking you to marry Dolly — that's your affair. Of course, it would gladden my heart and the heart of your poor, dead, sainted daddy and probably your mamma and anybody else knows what's right — but that's your affair. I'm just asking you now, as father to son, as a man without a country, come on over to Souick's and bring your ma."

Ike-o looked down at the ground and did not answer but finally let Fats move him toward the front door.

They went upstairs together and waited while Yolanda dressed herself, not talking to each other, Ike-o Hartwell looking down at the floor, unable to resist the persuasive intentions of Fats Smolcher. His mother was pleased with the prospect of attending a wedding reception at Souick's

Social Hall. "I'll bet I see people from when Grandma was a girl," she said happily.

Fats called a cab downstairs and grandly gave the driver a dollar tip when he delivered the three of them the seven blocks away where Souick's Social Hall stood on a small, clay embankment. It was a rare Saturday night in the old days that the police were not quelled by rioting well-wishers from Souick's who decided to extend the party to the rest of Sobaski's Stairway, but lately, the Negroes having their own clubs and ballrooms, the place had fallen into disuse. There hadn't been a riot there in ten weeks.

Fats chuckled inwardly watching Ike-o. "Like the moth and the flame, you know," he said later, submerged in the glow of self-congratulation and premium beer. He was hardly able to hold his head up from the table, but he was borne aloft by the knowledge of his own craft. Ike-o had stopped at the double wooden door blinking at the bright lights and noise of the three-piece band. Then Ike-o took his mother over to the wall around which sat other old women and left her with a Mrs. Pilsundski from over by Thirteenth in the old days, but living in the suburbs now with her kids, and Mrs. Helen Smola and Bernice Eugenko and Mrs. Stanley Kidd, all returned to Sobaski's Stairway for one big Saturday night honoring the marriage of one of Teddy Smolcher's daughters. The elderly women along the wall sat dressed in black as formal as at a funeral. Some of them along the wall tapped their feet to the drums. Later one or two of them might jump up and start to polka bearishly. Kids ran underfoot, knocking from the long tables pop and little cakes to the floor. Fats chuckled inwardly, watching Ike-o.

Ike-o blinked his eyes again and moved through the crowd. He moved directly on Dolly; her blonde head stood out above a small bobbing knot of people near the three-piece band. "Like the moth and the flame, you know," Fats said to himself, and then later to the world. Victory tasted momentarily good in his florid old jaws.

"Where's the medicine?" he whooped. "Teddy needs a drink."

The three-piece band played earnestly, the saxophone courageously carrying the melody while the bass player and the drummer chanted the lyrics and played their instruments.

> *I got a girl friend,*
> *She is a honey,*
> *She only loves me,*
> *When I got money.*

Ike-o did the polka with Dolly; he did not bark as some of the others did, but the hoopa-hoopa-yip-yip was inside him. She was the most beautiful woman in the hall and, even with cigarette smoke heavy and gray on the air, her blue eyes sang out for her loveliness. Ike-o smiled back at her and thought to himself that if she were a widow and had one kid it wouldn't make any difference or even if she were divorced it wouldn't make any difference. Or if she were a movie star and many men had slept with her there'd still be a million guys would want her if they knew for sure she'd love only them.

The saxophone carried the melody while the other two, a bald bass player and a bushy drummer, talked the lyrics.

> *I drink plain soda.*
> *She drinks her rock and rye,*
> *We'll be so happy,*
> *Julayda, you and I.*

They danced around the room, stamping their feet. Some of the dancers howled. "Hoop-a, hoop-a, hoop-a."

> *She says, "No, Johnny,*
> *Oh, no, don't squeeze me,"*
> *She says, "No, Johnny,*
> *Oh, no, don't tease me."*

Ike-o stopped Dolly near the door when the polka was over, holding her close as was the custom after a dance, but not releasing her. Someone came in and the cool air with him felt good. "Let's stand outside," Dolly said, and they went to stand out on the steps.

The air was friendly on their moist skins.

"I almost died when you walked up to me like that," Dolly said, "and said to me, 'May I have this dance!' — I had it promised but I couldn't say no to you. But I thought it was all over between us."

"I don't know what to tell you."

"You haven't seen me in five weeks."

"Don't have to tell me, I know."

They stood silently and then Dolly took his hand and

said, "Let's walk." They walked down to Mechanic Avenue and then down Mechanic.

"I know where we're going," Ike-o said.

"It's like we have to go."

"I know," Ike-o said, "we never should have stopped that other time. I wake up at night thinking about it."

"Do you, Ike-o? Do you?"

"Don't go for my sake," Ike-o said.

"It's me as much as you," Dolly said. "I felt like killing myself that night."

"Don't say that."

They walked upstairs to the apartment and Ike-o felt strangely cool, as if he were not with a woman at all but a man friend in the darkness. She opened the door to her place and did not turn on the lights but went to the kitchen and put on a pot with coffee. It was not heat but another excitement.

"I remember," she said, "when I was a kid and used to polka. All the time I was dancing I was watching myself too and I could be myself dancing and see myself dancing, my hair jumping on my head, and the men looking at my legs, and I thought I could do anything with them. There isn't another dance like the polka for seeing yourself."

"I saw you a long time ago," Ike-o said. "It was just like that, with your head tilted a little to help you laugh."

They stood silently in the kitchen; the small room was lit by the blue gas flame beneath the pot. The flame flecks wavered on the wall, finding the curve of a pitcher, the rim of a pan, a meaningless, flickering circle on the ceiling above the stove.

"When I pray too," Dolly said, "sometimes I used to see myself, kneeling there, my eyes closed."

"Were you pretty?" Ike-o asked.

"I don't know," she said, "it wasn't my face I saw, just my body there kneeling, my head down — I used to pray for you all the time."

"What?"

"Oh, that things would be good between us."

He pulled her to him and kissed her, not seeing her face in the blue gas-lit darkness, and picked her up and carried her to the bed and took off her party dress and white brassière and underpants and his own clothes while she lay with her eyes lidded, breathing gently. He pulled her to him and felt her beneath him and her moistness and warmth and released her and pulled her and himself together again. Then he heard the noise from the kitchen and thought of the coffeepot on the stove, gray and hot, and clutched her head and bit her lips and heard as distinctly as if it were a part of his ear the coffee boiling in the next room. And he felt a sadness because even the woman a man could love was only another woman in a bed: where had disappeared the Dolly of his dreams? He sank and rose and pounced again and galloped and raced and ran and felt he would die and burst and did and finally noticed that the heat and excitement had subsided with a cramp in his thighs. They lay apart and breathed heavily.

"I think the coffee's ready," Dolly said.

❖   ❖   ❖

Emma Carnavan tried to rouse Fats, but he would not let himself be jostled from his cozy dream, in which all of the women in the world had neatly paired with them in a long corridor all of the men along a short opposite wall. "Like the moth and the flame," he said to Emma, and he was happy there was only one more daughter to marry and in the corridor in his mind there waited a man for her. "Come on," Emma said, "someone took a lady's purse."

Life seemed reasonable to Fats Smolcher; he refused to investigate the missing purse and lifted his head only when he realized the band had stopped and that a woman was screaming. He stood unsteadily, peering through the cigarette smoke at the place near the door where the celebrators converged. It was Dolly screaming.

"Okay," Ike-o shouted, "okay."

Fats turned away. Years of habits from Sixth Street were not easily broken; with any of his other daughters screaming those fifty feet away, Fats would have leisurely strolled over to the men's room or to the small bar and had for himself a straight. Fats shuddered. He began to weep at the sight of his musicians putting up their instruments in their cases and putting them under the bandstands. They were good Polish boys all — Fats knew their families. He wept, with apprehension, not at the approaching battle but that his baby doll, his favorite, was in the middle of it.

In the smoke and in his alcoholic daze it was not easy for Fats to see well; and the sight was not anything a man would linger over. Ike-o had pursued Dolly to a far wall, shaking off the Catfish and other well-wishers, and had knocked her to the ground. From under his dark blue suit he had ripped an army belt he wore, and he beat Dolly with it as she crouched screaming beneath a latticed window. She tried jumping through the window but it was barred.

Fats tiptoed in his mind back to the happy corridor where a man waited for every woman in the world and especially his Dolly. It was him needed the strapping, not Dolly, Fats wept to himself. If he had been the right kind of father there wouldn't have been unloosed on the world all these hungry women and their mother to boot. But what else could anyone of done? Look at the tables loaded with food, his life savings spent on Rita — was there a better father anywhere? Fats wept for himself, a reasonable, orderly man in a suspicious, confusing, whorehouse world.

"There," Ike-o cried, "I been saving that for you for five weeks, the Catfish was right, they was all right about you. You're Sixth Street trash." He whipped at the things in himself that had made a pushover of him for this pretty face and long limbs. He struck desperately at her bare skin. He did not know when he was going to stop, maybe not until he had killed her and then himself.

Whether the explosion within Ike-o had come because Dolly danced or did not dance with someone else was never determined; or whether it had happened because of something she had said or not said or he had said and then answered himself freakishly, the details that brought up the violence were never clear even to Dolly and Ike-o. Two forces had stood arguing in Ike-o's mind as real as two men in black standing at a judge's desk, one standing and shouting and then sitting while the other man in black did the same thing. It did not matter that Dolly had an illegitimate son by another man, one would shout.

She was a tramp, fair game, now, forever, yesterday — and the child lived and breathed and proved it.

But what's past is past; there was no way to control the sins that had happened yesterday. Only now and ten minutes from now.

She'd do it again. The leopard can't change his spots.

In the murky middle ground in Ike-o's mind there erupted a violence and an answer of its own. She had not done right by him no matter what else; and he was going to punish his betrayer. Whether it was their entrance that had started it, her saying, "I feel like dancing," and him looking at her, only his eyes wild with the debate in his brain, and saying, "I don't feel like dancing," and then, "Okay if I dance with someone else?"

"You don't have to ask me," he had said, "we ain't married."

And the violence had brewed, like a thousand-year-old hatred born in the bricks of Sobaski's Stairway or coffee an hour ago in a condemned tenement.

Someone else had asked her to dance and she had turned to Ike-o waiting for an answer. When it came it was a battle cry thrust from the tortured middle ground in his mind where Ike-o had huddled up to this time in some kind of calm. "Okay," he shouted, "okay," answering a question of his own.

He took his belt and struck her first full in the face and

then punched her to the ground and spit on her. "Whore!" he cried. "Whore of Sobaski's Stairway!"

"Don't, Ike-o," she said, slipping to her knees.

"Here's the whore of Sobaski's Stairway," Ike-o shouted, striking her across the buttocks. "I'll get you." He pursued her across the napkin-strewn, polished floor of Souick's Social Hall.

The Catfish held him occasionally but was shaken off. It wasn't until someone grappled with his feet and brought him down that Ike-o looked out of eyes misty and red but sane again. "You were right, O. C.," he said, looking up, "the leopard don't change his spots."

He was helped to his feet and did not look at Dolly cowering across the room under the window but left with his mother and the venerable Gedunsky. They left in a silence as dark and gray as the cigarette smoke in the air; and with the start of the music voices became loud again. In ten minutes, Dolly having removed herself to the ladies' room, one could never have known it was not another Saturday night wedding reception at Souick's.

Percy Leech stayed on, dancing with the bride and making indecent suggestions to Rita. "Say, you," she said, "if I was a man I'd punch you in the nose suggesting an indecent thing like that to me on my wedding night."

"I'd give you something for your trouble," Percy said. "Remember, there was two other occasions."

"You ain't a gentleman," Rita said, breaking off the fox trot.

She went to find her dear daddy, who would beat the hell out of Percy Leech for her, but Fats sat staring at the

three-piece band in a comalike trance. He would not be
moved. And he ain't all that drunk, Rita thought, wondering about her father's mental state. She looked for her new
husband, thinking that Georgie would get a couple of his
Boston cousins and smack Leech alongside the ear, and
when she could not find Georgie she became panicky.

She searched everywhere, in the toilets and outside on
the clay embankment where the Social Hall stood, but it
wasn't until she looked under the bandstand that she found
her groom. She could not arouse him, poor Georgie, the
excitement had been too much for him; he had rolled from
a table and been shoved under the bandstand by a well-
wisher for safekeeping. It was a good thing Rita had missed
him and searched for him. He might have slept under the
bandstand for eternity for all anyone else had noticed him
gone. She dusted him off and wiped the spittle on his chin.

13

Miss Fireman did not outlive her dead building by long, a matter of five weeks, perhaps six. Ike-o had not seen her in her shack for four days and then heard thirty-six hours after it happened that she was dead. Spook Novakovitch said it was a damned shame but that everybody had to go sometime.

Miss Fireman died on a Tuesday night, in her hotel room in Oakland, among carpeted floors and pitchers with melting ice in them, the strange things, Ike-o thought, that she had avoided while she still breathed, searching out for herself trouble and for others comfort. "Not her, Spook," Ike-o said, "she didn't have to go ever."

"Yeah, sure," Spook said. He was called Spook because he was a mulatto, something of a human ghost drifting between the races; he said Ike-o was entitled to a free game of eight ball, sensing Ike-o's pain and not knowing anything else to say or do.

As it was the custom of Jews not to bury their dead

on a Friday, there was only one day and night of public mourning. It was the Thursday morning of her burial day that Ike-o heard the news.

"O. C.," he cried, running up Mechanic Avenue in army clothes, "Miss Fireman is dead!" He had left the poolroom to run home to change his clothes, but, once out in the sunlight of Mechanic Avenue, the mood seized him to run through the streets shouting his information.

"She's dead, O. C., she's dead, I heard it down the poolroom!"

O. C. Gedunsky, a tired Catfish, sat on a milk box before the Mechanic Avenue Police Station. "I heard," he said. "I heard. We'll put away our quarrel for a day. Go put on a white shirt, we'll go to the funeral."

In the bright July air O. C. Gedunsky mumbled no prayers. Ike-o watched him and could testify that as Miss Fireman's coffin was lowered into the ground the Catfish's jaws remained clamped shut, a muscle protruding under his cheek. A pale nephew stood at the foot of the grave and mumbled after the rabbi the kaddish, the Jewish prayer for the dead. The sunlight brought out all of their features boldly but flat and reliefless. Ike-o looked from face to face of the mourners, searching on the clean, white faces for a sign that someone understood the loss that had happened to the world thirty-six hours ago. He recognized none of the people — white shirts and ties and smelly perfume and black-dressed, corseted women, not a looker among them, double-chinned and reverently quiet and bored, even the rabbi and nephew. Only Gedunsky with his magnificent jaw clenched tight, hiding his pain under the swarthy tough flesh, and the leaden brain of Ike-o Hartwell bringing tears to his eyes, carried grief on the warm July afternoon. These were professional friends of Miss Fireman; and Ike-o supposed she had never been much account to these people. "She was a fine woman," he heard monotonously many times, and felt like spitting and swearing but held himself back until that night, when he was in Sobaski's Stairway.

"Tell me, O. C.," he asked, "how does it happen she can be put into the ground like that and there ain't one real thing different with the world?"

"It's final," Gedunsky said, "it's just final, there ain't nothing more emphatic." Ike-o stood with Gedunsky on the corner of Gardenia and Mechanic Avenue waiting for the crying feeling to pass again. It was not a warm night but buoyant and cool with the fall ahead, enough chill still in the air to make the darkness exhilarating.

"Why don't people talk more about it?" Ike-o asked.

"They ain't got the guts."

"It ain't good to think about," Ike-o said. "It's good people don't think about it till they're older. They got a little time to prepare."

O. C. Gedunsky closed his eyes. "I moved the blanket aside from a dead man's face once," he said. "I was fifteen maybe. I don't know what I expected to see, nobility maybe — sweet repose. I didn't know then that men don't die like men." He opened his eyes; he seemed startled to see Ike-o. "What a fool I was! That dead miner's face was broken up like a baby doll's. It was smeared and dirty with coal dust." He stood up and paced the street corner, his white head bent toward the ground to better analyze the young fool of fifty years ago. "I don't know what I expected to find under the cloth," he said with his back to Isaac. "It was indecent, unreasonable that a grown man should die with a dirty streaked face like a bad kid."

They stood for a few minutes contemplating the facts of life and were hardly aware that Percy Leech was shouting "Ike-o" and "Catfish" from two blocks away. He came running down the street waving his arms.

"Ike-o — Catfish." He was breathless.

"You like to go around shouting people's names in the street?" the Catfish asked. "You do it all the time?"

Percy Leech regained his frail composure. "Oh, sing it, Catfish," he said vehemently, "I got the news. You know a big celebrity like you can't keep things a secret in Sobaski's Stairway. When you leaving, Square-shake?"

"In about four days," the Catfish said mildly. "I'm kissing this place good-by for good."

Ike-o did not look at him; the world pulls in on itself, it ends, it suffocates itself like a match gone out, and Ike-o Hartwell stands on the corner of Mechanic and Gardenia and looks away and asks no questions and waits dumbly to suffer further.

O. C. Gedunsky sat down on a milk box, and Ike-o leaned on a telephone pole, looking down at him. It seemed to Ike-o that the cool Sobaski's Stairway night might go on forever: a streetcar sound, the silhouette of a beautiful colored girl crossing the street and blocking out twenty dollars' worth of green neon with her bouncing hips and bust, and the loose eternal laughter of street bums erupting and dying and sounding forth again.

"I guess it's time I took my leave," Gedunsky said.

"You didn't give me no notice," Leech said angrily. "You're damned lucky I heard about you going in time. Otherwise, my fine friend, you'd have gone by yourself — go find another barber like me."

"Percy," the Catfish said, "you wouldn't like where I was going."

"You implying something on my honesty?" Percy Leech asked.

"I ain't thinking about you," the Catfish said bluntly.

His brother Max in Denver, Colorado, knowing the great day was coming when O. C. would retire, had consolidated all of their investments into one mirrored and lacquered, polished bowling alley that grossed no less than seventy thousand a year. O. C. showed Ike-o and Percy colored picture postcards of the place; it looked plush.

"What makes you think I wouldn't like Denver, Colorado?" Leech asked.

"I'll see you before I go, Percy," the Catfish said, standing and taking Ike-o's arm. He steered Ike-o down Mechanic Avenue; neither looked back at Percy Leech still standing on the corner.

"Go to hell," Leech called. "I wouldn't be caught dead in Denver, Colorado."

"Can you imagine the tiger with civilized people?" Gedunsky asked, and then answered himself. "He got to go under with the buildings," he said, "but not me — life springs, you know, Ike-o. The Catfish got ninety-nine lives, don't look so sad."

Ike-o wished that the Catfish were not leaving Sobaski's Stairway, but then there would have to be no urban redevelopment, no Pennsylvania state redevelopment commission, no slum called for a dead moonshiner. But what of the nights? — Would there ever be nights as close, as friendly, as real to a person as the street-lighted Mechanic Avenue nights used to be in Sobaski's Stairway?

"Well, you still got your memories," Ike-o said, and then when the Catfish did not answer, "Well, don't you?" Ike-o sighed for good times gone.

"It's all over," the Catfish said, "there ain't even an echo of the shouting."

"I hate to hear you talk like that," Ike-o said, "it ain't like you, Catfish."

"You asked so I answered," the Catfish said, "but I'm far from dead. You know the Catfish, he got ninety-nine lives."

They shook hands on the dark, unlit corner where Seventh Street had been, Ike-o promising to look up the Catfish if he ever got to Denver, Colorado. "Next time I see you you'll be on a horse," Ike-o said.

"No," the Catfish said seriously, "they have cities there in Colorado just like here." He looked worried.

14

Out in East Liberty where Fats worked as a baker and bought his sausage he had a prospect. There wasn't a finger that fate had was brave enough to point a hex on Fats Smolcher's girls if their daddy would put himself out to find them a husband. He would stop in the man's butcher shop, tipping his hat, saluting, all cheerfulness and craft: "Well, Mr. Molyak, how's business this morning? — I ate them pork chops you sold me day before yesterday and I says to my old girl, 'Now a man who would sell a chop like that is a man I'd like to have for a friend.' It takes a good man to know meat I say and it takes a better man to sell it." Not to be put off, Fats waited until the butcher shop of Mr. Stefan Molyak was closed and walked with him to the corner. "Well, Mr. Molyak, it's nice to see the long day over, ain't it? — I don't drink myself, but I'd be proud to buy a countryman a drink." Fats nearly swooned with happiness when he learned that Mr. Molyak did not drink as well as bearing like a crown his widowerhood.

It developed from long conversations, sincere on Mr. Molyak's part, his eyes glistening with his loneliness and desire, and guile from Fats, his eyes too shining but with ambition and tiny clues flickering there with which daughter he would eventually stick Mr. Molyak, that the butcher was indeed searching for a wife.

"My daughter Irene," Fats began one afternoon, "is living away from home and she worries her ma and me when we think of her." Irene Smolcher had been away from home off and on again — once in a brief two-month marriage to a merchant seaman and once with a carnival — since she was fifteen. She was thirty-six that summer.

"She ain't a baby in age," Fats said, "she got a fine job in an office, but even a girl twenty-two years old is a baby to her ma and pa. We watched our little girls like the eyes in our head. Fine, respectable girls, especially my Irene. She ain't missed a communion from a little girl." Fats did not know exactly what Irene did for a living. "She's living away from home now, and you'd do a father a real favor to look her up and maybe talk to her."

"I am not a forward person," Mr. Molyak said. "I would make a bad first impression."

Mr. Molyak was small and wiry with huge knotted forearms. His hands were large; they hung on the ends of his forearms like tools and looked empty when they were not grasping a cleaver or bone. He walked with his shoulders straight, eyes forward, hardly looking at Fats. He presumed that the elderly baker wanted him to marry one of his daughters; he was not unwilling if the girl was respectable.

"These girls have been brought up to respect people,"

Fats said. "Let me get you and Irene together. She's a peach, reads all the time, talk a leg off you — excuse me, you like a girl who can talk good? keep you in stitches? good looking? — yes, sir, by Jesus, excuse me, good looking."

"Oh, yes," Mr. Molyak said.

But he insisted there was to be no face-to-face introduction. First he was to observe Irene Smolcher, perhaps learn something about her, then if his impression was not unfavorable he would not think unkindly of Mr. Smolcher if a tea, a conversation, a prenuptial discussion would take place. The three times damned Irene had no phone, and twice when Fats went to her Northside apartment he could not find her; and when he finally found her in one night she was too stewed to make sense but seemed to understand that he was bringing a prospect to observe her. "And wear plenty make-up for cry-I," he exclaimed. Irene Smolcher looked not twenty-two but fifty-two.

Irene assured him as best she could that she would be home Sunday night.

Mr. Molyak and Fats arrived punctually at eight o'clock. The future bride was to make an appearance at eight-thirty, pause briefly to buy a *Post-Gazette* at the corner newsstand, and then continue on down Federal Street. Mr. Molyak and Fats stood in a cigar store and waited; Fats boasted of her regular habits — his daughter was at that minute probably putting on her coat to leave a church club. They stood in the doorway of the cigar store waiting.

"She was a real intelligent kid," Fats said, and again

for the fourth time, "A fortuneteller told us, while Marg was carrying her, that this kid was going to be the wife of a great man. A gypsy — knew everything about us, our names, our addresses, ages, didn't miss a thing and said Irene was going to be married to a great man."

Stefan Molyak sighed. "I am a plain man," he said.

"Ha," Fats laughed, "ha, ha, ha."

Mr. Molyak and Fats made nervous small talk, both casually sipping on bottles of soda pop, occasionally moving aside to allow customers to enter and leave. Molyak was quiet, glancing up from under his brows to gaze across the street as if a dream of love itself would walk down Federal Street and pause for a moment at the newsstand and then continue into his life instead of a washed-out daughter of Fats Smolcher.

"Irene was the one the nuns said should have taken the veil," Fats said, running short of virtues for her. He hardly remembered her; he had not seen much of her in the past fifteen years and the few times he saw her she had some jam to unravel. Once he had given her forty dollars.

"A person could get killed standing in a doorway over here on the Northside," Molyak said.

Fats chuckled. "All decent working people," he said.

A policeman passed, checked their identifications, and moved on. "We're visiting my daughter ain't come home yet," Fats had said proudly, and called after the policeman, "Goodnight, officer."

"Nice fellow," he said to Molyak because they had not been arrested.

At eleven thirty, Stefan Molyak said, "I'm stiff from standing. I am going home."

"She must be at a friend's house," Fats said cautiously. "She works every day. She ain't missed a day in years. I can't understand where she'd be at this hour."

However, they decided to wait another ten minutes, then fifteen minutes more.

At twelve o'clock the cigar store was closed, and Fats, Mr. Molyak, and some boys who were playing a pinball machine were turned out. "She must have broke a leg," Fats said bitterly.

"Is it possible?" Mr. Molyak asked.

Fats persuaded him to drive to her apartment, and Fats went upstairs in the building, an old mansion with charred black pillars and decaying steps. He came back to say, "She'll be in in a few minutes, there's a friend up there waiting for her."

There were, in fact, two friends waiting for Irene Smolcher, both men, both drunk, but only one of them with pants. The man without pants was crawling around on his knees searching for Irene or his pants, whichever one should miraculously appear first out of the alcoholic vistas that enshrouded Irene Smolcher's third-floor hall. "A nice old lady bringing my kid some soup," Fats mumbled. "My Irene tended her when she was sick."

When Irene appeared it was too dark to see her.

"Honey," Fats called, "oh, honey-dear, don't be frightened, it's me your daddy."

She came toward the car, wobbling on four-inch heels but keeping her balance by tilting neatly backward. "Who's there?" she called.

Fats held Mr. Molyak's forearm tightly when he clutched the steering wheel. "Don't be shy, Steve, don't be shy," he whispered pleadingly, "she's just plain folks like us — she's just plain folks."

Irene fell against the car, bumping her head on the window glass. "There's a rock there," Fats exclaimed, stepping out and holding open the door with one hand and Irene with the other. "It's mighty dark out," Fats said bravely. "Miss Irene Smolcher, this is Mr. Molyak, an old friend of Daddy's — Stevie, this is one of my dear little girls."

"Pleased to meet you," Irene said, poking her head into the darkness of the car.

Mr. Molyak's interior lights were not working; but he did not hesitate. He had come to observe and, since that was the bargain, freely entered into by both parties, observe he would. He flicked on a cigarette lighter; and Irene grinned a blackened and foolish smile at the new whirling light, her eyes wandering far, then near. She had not worn enough powder or it had disappeared in her evening's adventures; the face was of a dead-white tiredness and drunken and used. Mr. Molyak snapped shut his cigarette lighter.

He did not talk to Fats until they came to Sobaski's Stairway, where Fats had him drop him off on Mechanic Avenue. Mr. Molyak had not until that evening ever thought there was anything strange about his matchmaker. Now he wondered where the man lived, had he a home? There were certainly no houses within ten blocks.

"Huh?" Fats asked dumbly when Stefan Molyak said bitterly, "I want no more of your matchmaking. I am going to die a widower. I want no more matchmaking."

Fats said nothing further. Tomorrow was another day, and Fats Smolcher had one more eligible daughter.

"Well," Fats said with bravado, "I guess even an old dog like me got to learn new tricks." When there was no answer he said, sadly, "My kid took to drink since she's been away from home, Mr. Molyak. Look what a year can do to a person."

"She didn't even have real blonde hair," Mr. Molyak said bitterly, pulling shut the door to his coupé and driving away to leave Fats standing alone under a street light. "It takes all kinds to make a world," Fats said inside of Cohen's with a sigh of great philosophical mystery. He was not discouraged.

As luck would have it, Dolly was bathing her baby when Mr. Molyak with Fats at his elbow knocked at her door. She came to the door, carrying the boy in a light blanket. Fats had told Mr. Molyak that the two children Dolly tended were his own; he had hoped to be able to make a fuller explanation after he had Stefan Molyak entangled. But Molyak stood at the door staring at Dolly and then the baby, and Fats could not push past him. "This gentleman here — " Fats started, but Molyak stood rooted on the rotten wooden floor, looking from the mother to the child.

"Well, what are you gaping at?" Dolly asked.

"This gentleman here — " Fats began again.

"This is no single girl," Mr. Molyak said. "This baby is hers."

"This gentleman here," Fats said, "is interested in matrimony and we're in no position to be particular." The urgency of the moment appealed to Fats Smolcher; he would heroically save the situation, damn the obstacles, babies, chance. "We have a few things we must discuss," Fats said. "There's no reason for anyone to run off with half of the facts."

Dolly slammed the door on both of them. "Get out," she said through the door, "or I'll call a cop."

"She will, too," Fats said. "I know her."

Outside, where Fats could see Stefan Molyak's face in the daylight, he saw that the hard little man's silence was not anger but a sort of amazement. He had been surprised.

"I want your daughter, Mr. Smolcher," Stefan Molyak said. "She is the most beautiful woman I ever saw."

Percy Leech had persuaded a girl of his own to walk the streets for him. She was a fifty-three-year-old drunk who had been away for several nerve cures too but always came back from Louisville with a stronger craving for drugs. Percy ignored completely O. C. Gedunsky sitting at the front door by the night light in Cohen's Restaurant.

There had developed a distance and seemingly irreparable coolness between Leech and Gedunsky since the Catfish had left for Denver without taking Leech with him; and when the Catfish came back, looking like a shaggy, underfed dog someone had booted, Percy Leech took it as a vindication. He refused to talk to the Catfish.

Gedunsky bowed after him. "Good evening, your majesty," he said. But Percy Leech was too busy to reply, apparently too absorbed to answer menials. However, his financial well-being with his girl was still in the future.

His hustler currently gave him not a dime a week — his steady income came from a newspaper stand he worked out on the Northside.

He enjoyed the importance of sidling up behind men at Cohen's crap game and whispering, "I know where there's a young divorcee twenty-nine years old can't contain herself. A tenner will get you an invite." He'd accept a deuce or a buck and a half and give it all to his girl friend, too timid to keep any of the money for himself.

Behind his back, the Catfish made bitter signs. He sat every night at the front door, a bent, broad-shouldered man with deep thoughts, and stood reluctantly to open the door for each new arrival. He was not to admit strangers or policemen; if the place was raided it was an unspoken agreement between doormen and operators that the doorman would take the fall. There was a button to press on the police that buzzed Nate Cohen's office to the rear of the restaurant and game. The game was not likely to be raided; it was peanuts.

"I thought you had something good in Denver," Ike-o said, at first sympathetic and then with no kindness. "Big talk is all you ever were."

O. C. Gedunsky, from his moral position somewhere on the floor near the spittoon, would nod. "I went for thirty thousand dollars' worth of picture postcards. I followed Max out to California, but I lost him there."

"Serves you right," Ike-o said.

"I wish I'd have found him," the Catfish said thoughtfully, ruminating among the odds and ends of his life where at intervals he had commanded the homage of thousands and now would not get respect from a Gardenia Street punk, "I'd have introduced Max to a small lead pipe I was carrying as payment for the postcards."

They both knew their luck had to change, and silently sat waiting by the night light over the steam ovens, occasionally rising to go into the back room and gaze hungrily on the money being exchanged, only to return more desperately to the front door to wait for lightning to strike. Outside, the street disappeared under bulldozers and cranes while O. C. and Ike-o waited.

On a Saturday night, the eviction notice for the restaurant already in O. C.'s breast pocket and sadness in their chests, a drunken Fats Smolcher staggered into Cohen's. Fats, who was not much of a gambler, stood unsteadily eating a corned beef sandwich and watching the crap game in the back room. He did not speak to Ike-o, who stood at a far corner of the dice table.

"Say, you," Ike-o said, "you got the manners of a pig. Go eat out on the counter. We don't want to watch you eat."

Fats pushed the rest of the sandwich into his mouth and snatched the dice from the center of the table; he sensed the men around the crap table were with him. He rattled the dice and then stopped. Fats held them over his head, not looking at Ike-o, and said, "When I gamble I concentrate on what I'm doing — I wish The House would quiet the noisemaker."

"You mean me, Fats?" Ike-o asked.

"I mean you, punk."

Gedunsky put his hands on Ike-o's arm. "Keep your

mouth shut, Isaac," he said, "or stand outside. You ain't gambling."

"Who says I ain't — what are you shooting, Whorehouse John?" In Ike-o's pocket were two monthly payments of a hundred dollars toward his father's statue. He had not been able to bring himself to give the money to Sladic. He still needed an additional hundred dollars. But he took the money from his pocket and waved it at Fats.

"Put your money where your mouth is," Ike-o called.

Fats held in his pocket some three hundred dollars which he had acquired that afternoon from the sale of Mr. Molyak's 1948 Ford. He did not expect that any of the money would be risked if he were to take it from his pocket, hold it aloft carelessly with one meaty hand while rattling the dice in the other, and shout, "I got a son-in-law to stake me, Mr. Hartwell, I got plenty of money."

"Who, Georgie Grinnek?"

Neither of them thought at that moment that the argument would progress any further, but Fats answered back, "I got more than one daughter, punk." He had already conceived of Dolly as safely married to Stefan Molyak, had insinuated himself to where he was acting as a middleman in various other transactions for Mr. Molyak, and the last thing he wanted to do was to incite Ike-o about Dolly. He hoped that was over. Ordinarily he would have thrown something at his tormentor and left, but Dolly had been mentioned and her honor was again afloat on the cigarette smoke of Cohen's back room.

"You can't mean a certain tramp I know?" Ike-o asked.

"You're out of line," O. C. Gedunsky said, again taking

Ike-o by the arm. "That ain't no way to talk," Percy Leech said, hoping something would start. He bristled and so did several others.

"I'm shooting one hundred dollars," Fats said, and threw down on the table two fifty-dollar bills. "If the punk ain't gambling, I wish somebody would escort him out."

Ike-o put up the money, and Fats, licking his lips, his eyes amazed while they bolted around the room, rattled the dice and threw a three, a two and a one showing.

"Nut balls, too small to call," Percy Leech chanted. The game had no stickman. Leech had appointed himself arbiter.

"Well," Fats said, watching the money going with Hartwell, the green felt of the table empty. "Well, well, well."

"It's still your dice," Ike-o said, "or don't you have the courage of your convictions, John?"

Fats won fifty dollars back on a seven, lost another hundred on a twelve, rolled a six, and then rolled a four, an eight, and sevened out. Ike-o picked up the dice and threw down a hundred dollars. An amazed Fats faded him as a seven came up. The exchange took six minutes. Ike-o waved the two hundred and fifty dollars he had won.

"You bought my old man his statue," Ike-o cried, as astonished as Thaddeus Smolcher.

"You shut up," Fats shouted, seizing a Coca-Cola bottle. "Your old man's in hell, where he belongs."

"Take it back," Ike-o said, "take it back." He picked up a bottle by the neck and held it menacingly.

The venerable Gedunsky cleared his throat. The purity of his good intentions shone in the hollow from under his white eyebrows. "You're acting like cannibals," he said.

"I said for Hartwell to shut up," Fats screamed. "For him to shut up about me, about my daughter, about everything. I been listening to his fake old man for forty-five years, and, no disrespect to the dead, but he was the biggest bastard fourflusher in Sobaski's Stairway and his son is another one just like him. I laid his father in a sewer down on Thirteenth Street, near Spook Novakovitch's place, for calling me personally a bad name, reflecting on the Polish people, and I will do the same to the son if he wants to make trouble."

It was Fats who left with feeling running against him for speaking unkindly of the dead. He sensed antagonism in the silence in the room and thundered out. Some of the men later swore that he had mumbled, or shouted — the curse was that uncertain — that he would smash the statue of Charlie Hartwell. But his talk as he walked out was of smashing and anger and busting something to pieces, Sobaski's Stairway, Ike-o Hartwell. It was never certain that Fats had uttered a threat against the huge Jesus which was to stand over Charlie Hartwell's grave. "Get out of here, Isaac," Gedunsky said, "we don't need no troublemakers."

Ike-o paid off the statue the next day, describing for young Sladic the location of the grave from directions which Yolanda had written on an envelope. "You got you one good bargain," Sladic said, and shook hands on the deal.

Ike-o went to the Catfish to offer to be friends; things for him, at least, were right. "Keep your hand in your pocket," O. C. said. "I don't need no parts of you." Ike-o avoided him, left him to sit sullenly at his front door, a stooge in his old age where he had once been king. The Catfish hated everyone, all of humanity, "down to the Chinks I ain't met yet," he said, expressing contempt for them all as potential Judases. He talked little to anyone, and one August day the Catfish went outside on the sidewalk of Cohen's with Ike-o and a group of motley strangers and stood with his eyes liquid and fixed, and watched as a crew of men in yellow helmets pulled down the building which had given shelter to Cohen's Restaurant, the last indoor crap game in Sobaski's Stairway. Nate Cohen was not there to see it. He had given O. C. Gedunsky his last week's wages, hustled his wife aboard a plane South, and retired to Miami. It was left to the Catfish to juggle the key to the joint, tossing it once lightly into the air, and then to heave it like a wreath onto the rubble.

"Crap game convenes four o'clock this afternoon at the Bible institute," he said loudly, and started up Mechanic Avenue toward the Police Station. He had been provided a temporary cot there and made the place his home.

The game wasn't held that afternoon. It rained.

15

"It runs in the family," Emma Carnavan said to Dolly, glad to have company. "You Polish people like to sing."

Dolly turned down the music on Emma's radio. "It's the last thing I feel like doing," she said. "I'm not singing out of happiness." The bright, crowded old bus, the music reverberating around the walls, the children playing on the floor, it was for rightness she hummed along with the radio, not happiness — that was too much to ask. Just rightness.

She shivered, remembering the night before, the hands of Purbanko the contractor, the hulking nose, the eyes burning in the darkness of her hallway. He had walked with her down Mechanic Avenue, leading her little sister by the hand innocently, while Dolly carried her son Richard. He had seemed big and harmless and shy in his straw hat. He spoke of a cousin who was infatuated with her and in the old-country fashion had sent him to plead with her for a date. He had himself only tonight worked up the nerve to talk to her.

She had walked along, talking to him, and stopped him downstairs in the hallway, but smiled at him and said, "Thanks, I'll see you again," and tried to close the door.

"There's no one living here," he said. "This ain't a building for a nice girl like you." His eyes glowed like his cigar; and Dolly knew that the cousin did not exist and the man with the terrible feeling for her was this big, quiet, crafty man blocking her door. "I ain't going to let you walk in these dark hallways yourself," he said, and she could not stop him but let him walk with her up the steps. She could not hear his breathing and knew he controlled it and this frightened her.

"No further," she said at the door, not seeing him or hearing him either in the darkness.

She felt his hands around her, pulling her close, and smelled the cigar on his mouth. He kissed her face and she screamed.

"Don't," he said. "Don't."

She clawed at his face, stumbling over her baby and her little sister, crawling away and kicking at him as she fell. She heard him swear and then his footsteps as he ran down the steps. "Two-bit whore," he called, while she leaned against the door sobbing.

"Why?" she asked the children and the darkness. "Why?"

The next morning she made her decision, coming from her apartment with the children, preparing to take them up Mechanic Avenue to the bus where Emma would watch them. In the hallway she stopped to pick up the little red and black metallic package. The man had had no opportunity to unwrap the prophylactic, but it had been in his hand with his cigar, casually, unconcerned, as if there was no need to stop puffing his cigar or to ask her before he used her. The contractor was afraid of catching a disease from her. "Goddamn him," Dolly said softly, meaning at least one more man than Conrad Purbanko. "How long does it take a woman to get wise?" she asked Emma.

"You ask me, they never do," Emma Carnavan said.

Mr. Molyak seated himself in the room's one chair; it was burgundy colored and mohair and overstuffed, and, being a small man, Mr. Molyak sank uncomfortably into its deep springed recesses. Tilting himself like a small jack-knife from the hips, he pulled himself forward by the arms. Mr. Molyak was conscious of his size and was determined to allow no adversary an advantage.

"I am a plain man," he stated, "and I talk plain. I am a very plain man, Miss Smolcher — I do not put on a big act."

"He means he's no phony, Doll, honey," Fats said, shifting from foot to foot. "He means he's an honest man."

Mr. Molyak held up his hand precisely like a policeman stopping traffic. "Stefan Molyak does not need an interpreter," he said, "thank you, for myself. I have brought the father of the prospective bride here so that there will be no question of promises that have been made and not fulfilled. I will speak plainly — I will put all my cards on the table."

Dolly went to the window and stared at the blank wall across the narrow courtyard. She held a small white handkerchief and ground it into a ball.

"I am fifty-one years old," Mr. Molyak said. "I have good habits. I play golf like any American on Sunday mornings — I go to an early Mass; I am very regular in my habits."

"By golly, that's the way I like to hear a man talk," Fats said, glancing up at Dolly standing across the room.

"I have my own business," Mr. Molyak said. "I am a member of the Chamber of Commerce in East Liberty. My credit is excellent."

"There's nothing like good credit," Fats said hesitantly.

"Now I am no child, Miss Smolcher," Mr. Molyak said, standing and walking to where she stood but then changing his mind. He stepped backward two long paces when he saw the obvious difference in their sizes; Dolly was several inches taller than Mr. Molyak.

"I am no child, Miss Smolcher," Mr. Molyak said. "I realize that I must not seem like such a big bargain to a young girl, but there is never a little give without a little take. You are not such a big bargain maybe to somebody else — but in the heart of Stefan Molyak the past is a closed book. I will ask no questions, just no froufrou when a woman is married to Stefan Molyak. That I will not tolerate. I am a former president of the East Liberty Chamber of Commerce — my credit is excellent. I am not a motorcycle rider."

"Are you proposing to me or asking me to go into business with you?" Dolly asked.

Fats laughed in hearty, false gusts, but Mr. Molyak did not smile. He said after a while, "A sense of humor is very valuable in a mate."

"Thanks," Dolly said.

Mr. Molyak took her by the elbow gingerly. "It is not altogether a proposition like a black and white contract," he said. "I have the instincts of a boy of seventeen — I am a plain man, I will not fool you on that. I will expect to live with you like any young man. I am a butcher. Our profession is physical, you know what I mean." He coughed and looked away as if to deny his manhood by the angle of his face. "It has been fifteen years since my wife died," he said, "and I have had no desire to marry again. It was not a good experience, Miss Smolcher. My late wife was a religious woman, a very, very religious woman, a good woman, maybe a saint, but she did not understand men. I am no saint, Miss Smolcher, I am a plain healthy man."

"He does the work of two men in his shop," Fats said, and held his breath. "And he doesn't drink!" Fats burst out. "He doesn't touch a drop."

There was quiet in the room, over which a clock ticked. A toilet was flushed somewhere in the building; water roared through pipes, the floor shuddered.

"Your father is accurate," Mr. Molyak said. "I do not indulge in liquors. It was a last request of my mother. She died three years ago. I have been very lonely for three years since she died."

Dolly sighed. Her arms were crossed under her chest, but she held them so tightly against herself that she might have been in a lover's embrace.

"I can understand loneliness, Mr. Molyak," Dolly said.

"I will make you a good husband," Mr. Molyak said.

"He sure will, honey," Fats cried. "Make it a go, Doll! Tell him, 'Okay, old boy.'"

Mr. Molyak recovered from a moment of weakness. He had been fondling in his hip pocket a wallet where there rested a picture of his mother; and in his loneliness and need for sympathy he had almost pulled out the faded snapshot and showed it to the girl. He wished someday he could tell a wife of how he had loved his mother and make her love the dead woman too.

Mr. Molyak held up his hand, again to quiet the charging Fats.

"A minute, Mr. Smolcher," he said calmly. "I said with every give there must be a little take. I have stated my side of the bargain — I have told you of my take. For to give I have an insurance policy for twenty thousand dollars. I have no family but a sister and her I hardly know, she lives in New Jersey. I will give my regular hours and a very plain religious man. An honest man."

"What are your terms, Mr. Molyak? What do you want of me?"

"Aw, that ain't no way to talk, Dolly," Fats said.

"You stay out of it, Dad," Dolly said.

"Good!" Molyak exclaimed. "This is a businesslike way to do things. We are both not children."

Dolly paced around the room, thinking, unable to talk until she knew herself what she wanted to say.

"All the buzzing comes to one thing, Mr. Molyak, that is my son," Dolly said. "What of him?"

"I will raise him like my own," Mr. Molyak said unhesitantly. "If God is good there will be others too. That is what I want from you — I want children. I am fifty-one and I have missed too much. I will raise your child like my own. His name will be Molyak."

Then for Dolly the questions, the pauses and doubts, the fear of this muscular little man evaporated. What more was there to ask? — everything had been answered. At nineteen Dolly Smolcher was very tired. This Stefan Molyak, the butcher with good credit, promised her a rest.

"I'll marry you," Dolly said, "tell me when."

Percy Leech and O. C. Gedunsky came to Ike-o's apartment door the following Sunday morning. They knocked primly, and, when Ike-o answered, he invited them in. "Put her there, pal," Leech said, taking Ike-o's hand and shaking it. Ike-o shook hands with both of them.

"What's the occasion?" Ike-o asked.

"My buddy and me are going for a fresh start in Miami Beach, Florida," Percy Leech said proudly. "We came to say good-by and no hard feelings."

"I got nine hundred and ninety-nine lives," the Catfish said.

"Ah, that old boy loves the water murky, Ike-o," Percy Leech said. "That's why they call him the Catfish, not because he used to feed the poor people fish food on national holidays, but because he likes the water muddy just like his namesake. He always got something in the fire."

The Catfish shrugged. "It ain't much," he said, "but it's a start. We're going to be driving cabs until a fellow I know can work us in as desk clerks in his hotel."

"I'd like to go with you," Ike-o said, "but I got my mother."

Outside gray rain mocked Ike-o's dream of starting somewhere all over again, fresh, wet, ready to be dried and striding forward boldly to be like everyone else. The rain made small streams that twisted into the dirt of Sobaski's Stairway and washed away by unhappy pieces the barren muddy earth. There were no beginnings for Ike-o Hartwell, only endings; he wanted the rain to change him, to cleanse him of things that seemed to grow with him like barnacles on an unclean ship.

"This ain't an invite," Leech said. "Maybe later, not now."

"I'll be the oldest cab driver in the Western Hemisphere," Oscar Gedunsky said, "but it's better than nothing."

"When are you leaving?"

"In a couple of hours," Leech said.

"Look," Ike-o explained, "I'm taking my mother out to the cemetery today to see the statue of my old man. Why don't you wait around till tonight? Come on, how about it?"

They agreed to meet again that night, and later Ike-o and Yolanda took a taxicab in the rain out to the cemetery where Charlie Hartwell was buried.

His anticipation of the visit to the grave was spoiled by Yolanda's eyesight. She had continually refused to have the cataracts removed from her eyes. But someone would have to be really blind not to see the way Ike-o Hartwell had taken care of his father's memory. He felt good, thinking that when his debt was paid he could say, like Gedunsky, that he had ninety-nine lives. Thus far there was only one life and it gave him damned little to brag about, he thought.

The rain came in intervals through the afternoon. The sky hung low and gray over the cemetery. They both carried raincoats over their arms because, while it was only September, the uncultivated ground was already soggy with leaves.

A late summer heat was in the air. They walked on the wet leaves and caught at each other as one, then another, slipped and righted themselves. "Take your time," the cab driver called. His meter ticked, and he took out a newspaper to read.

Ike-o hoped the sun would come out and fall on the statue so Yolanda would see it in all its importance and power. But as he pointed down over the hill to where it stood, Yolanda, gasping for breath after climbing on the wet ground, could only shake her head. She could see nothing down below.

Ike-o almost ran the last hundred yards to see the spectacle. This was his first view of the statue after Sladic had installed it. The statue stood as majestic and proud as it had been, but where the head had been was a ragged edge at the neck. Someone, probably Fats Smolcher, had knocked off the head of the Jesus and left it to sit peacefully and calmly at the feet of the robed statue. It was a ferocious revenge on the dead Charlie and his son. Ike-o caught his breath and waved Yolanda back.

But Yolanda would not stop. She could see only enough to know that the statue was big and white. She cried happily, not seeing that the figure was headless. "Let me touch it," she asked softly, and Ike-o led her hand to the white marble of the robe. "There," she said, satisfied, "it's everything Charlie and me wanted. Thanks, Ike-o. You made things good."

It did not seem important to Ike-o that Fats had knocked the head of the Jesus off or whether the statue had been cracked in transportation. The head could be fastened on again.

What intrigued him was that at the moment he should stand before his father's grave with his mother there should be imperfection, maybe hatred; there should be over the three of them a sense of something gone wrong. They were like people under a dark, unlucky star.

Yolanda wept soundless tears looking at the statue. "That's just about the way things run," Ike-o finally said, and took Yolanda's arm as if to help her up the wet hill. She released herself gently.

"Things started right and ended right, everything's right that ends right," she said. "This was the way it begun with Charlie and me and this was the way it ended. You made things right for me and Charlie, Isaac." Ike-o helped her on with her raincoat as a light rain started.

"Let's go," Ike-o said.

Yolanda stood with a small smile, her unseeing eyes focused nowhere but on her memories. "When Charlie and me got married," she said, "there wasn't a person in Greendale, Polish or not, who didn't wish us the best." She thought of the wedding they might have had with dancing all night and everyone throwing a donation into an apron to dance with the bride, but she had said "yes" to Charlie Hartwell and that meant marriage by a Presbyterian minister and no dancing and a lousy drink or two for the guests. But Charlie managed to get stewed anyhow and slept away her wedding night. Well, she had been to encugh Polish weddings, and one more couldn't have made that much difference. The rain ran down the valleys in her gross face. She did not brush it away. The rain was cool.

"I wasn't fat back then," she said, still smiling, "and Charlie was as straight as a pole. He had a good job, too, in maintenance, down at the railroad car company. In the first year we bought ourselves a Victrola on time, and don't think I wasn't the envy of my sisters. My man was a clerk, not a mill hunky, no sir."

When she did not talk, the rain could be heard gently falling on the leaves. She paused as if listening. "Then hard times come," she said, "and Charlie lost all our savings, but it wasn't money throwed away foolishly. Time wasn't right for some of Charlie's ideas — my God, that man had a brain in his head. You remember that big metal cabinet that used to sit down in the cellar on Gardenia Street until somebody stole it — you used to play on it when you was a kid, Isaac. That cabinet was an incinerator, and with a little bit of luck Charlie would have sold one to every house in Greendale, maybe in Pennsylvania. He had the whole state, yes, sir, the company what made them things gave Charlie Hartwell the whole state of Pennsylvania to sell their home incinerator in. If it would have caught on like television we'd all be millionaires now, but I guess people never will get tired of walking out to the garbage. The company went out of business in 1929 without even the good intentions to leave someone at their office to answer their mail. I can tell you Charlie wrote them some letters, but it never did much good. It broke his heart, he was never the same. You wouldn't think a swell idea like that wouldn't catch on, would you?"

"I think we better go," Ike-o said, "it's raining harder."

Yolanda put out her hand to touch the statue again. "My," she said. "I'll bet Charlie's tickled with me now."

She answered a challenge she had presented herself. "I

ain't saying everything was a bed of roses between us," she said. "I'm only saying there was enough good to kind of balance off the bad. He was no easy man to live with, no sir, not when he was boozing or coming off a tear. He was just about as unhappy as a man could be, I guess it must have been like glass in his throat after it was over and he was ashamed."

Standing out here in a cemetery in the rain reminded Yolanda of so many things: of little girls walking before the carriage with the horse where Iron Jake Stanachek lay dead and the little girls sprinkling rose petals as the procession went from the church to the Polish graveyard. That somehow made an honor of death, not mud and rain and the way Charlie Hartwell died, not like a gentleman in bed but drunk and with no rose petals strewn before him and a priest chanting the burial prayer. "Well, it's all over," she said. "He probably forgives us now."

Ike-o could not bear his mother's pain. "You got it wrong," he said. "There's nothing he ever had to be mad about."

Yolanda raised her hand again as if to wave at Ike-o. "I lived with him a long time, Isaac," she said, "and I done everything the way I thought he wanted it. A Polish woman takes plenty from a man before she lets loose." The soft rain fell on the wet ground; it ran down the face of the Jesus head, running along the nose as if the face were human, but then raggedly dripping off the tilted, severed neck.

"I knowed him," Yolanda said. "I was his wife. But you was just a kid, Isaac, you didn't ask for him for a father." She stopped to hear the rain, judging herself by its even patter. "I fell as low as one person could," she said, and twisted up her old, fat face; it would have been comical but for the raw pain there.

She began to weep. She leaned against the statue's robes like an ungainly, stricken child. The marble was wet, but she put her arm against it and bent her head forward. She covered her eyes and cried into her arm. "Dear Jesus, Son of Mary," she sobbed, "there ain't nothing You don't know so there's no keeping back my crime from You any more. You know what I had in my heart that night. I ain't asking for mercy, I don't deserve it. You ain't likely looked into a heart as black as mine."

Ike-o put his arm around her shoulder.

"I want You to know it all, though," she wept. "Maybe there was a corner in my heart even You couldn't see into. A door locked between Charlie and me might not mean what it does in every other case. I had murder in my heart mostly, dear Jesus, You know that. I was overflowing with hate that night, but when I saw him pale and needing a shave and dying, dear God, I knew it was only one more time I had locked Charlie out. I hadn't intended to kill him, I couldn't have loved him that much seeing him half dead that way. I locked that door to the apartment house because I was tired. Is that murder, dear God? Is being tired the same as hating?"

Ike-o held her closely, himself weeping.

"I locked him out in the storm," Yolanda said. "I murdered him because I was tired, I was tired of him coming into my house and raising hell. I was tired. He died of pneumonia, Isaac, you can ask them at the hospital how I killed him. A Polish woman waits a long time."

"We're wet clean through," Ike-o said. "It's time to go."

"Of all them people in our apartment house who knew Charlie and all the people on Gardenia Street," she said, "there wasn't one who would open their door to him. He died like a dog on the street. He was found in a pile of snow over his head, and I was the person who put him there." The rain splashed in a small puddle below the ragged neck of the broken marble head of Jesus.

"Oh, Charlie," Yolanda wailed, "why couldn't things have been different?" The muddy gray sky where she turned her sightless eyes pulsated evenly, rhythmically, unthinking. "Do you forgive us, Charlie?" she asked. "We forgive you, don't we, Isaac, don't we forgive?"

"Yes," Ike-o said, looking with her at the muddy sky. "It's all over, I forgive."

When they drove back the rain fell more heavily. Only in Sobaski's Stairway, devoid of buildings and streets, did the cab proceed with any speed. The cab driver's fee was eleven dollars and thirty cents, and Ike-o gave the patient driver a dollar tip.

In the apartment, Yolanda sat down heavily with as leaden a plunge as if she would not rise again. "I ain't going to like to leave Sobaski's Stairway, this apartment," Yolanda said. "It has happy memories for me."

Ike-o had persuaded her that the time had come to move to an apartment in Oakland. He dangled Mrs. Kavoris and Bernice Eugenko, who too lived with a son, as bait; they lived in Oakland and promises had been made, good wishes extended, that they would all resume old friendships in Oakland as if that old and decaying neighborhood were the promised land.

"I'm going to feel like I'm leaving Charlie when we leave here," Yolanda said sadly. "I don't want to leave Charlie, Isaac. He gave us some happy times."

"Okay," Ike-o said, "don't cry no more, Ma."

"Once a week maybe he'd come home with something he stole in his shirt," Yolanda said. "He'd make me guess what it was. We'd play like two kids — once it was two trout fish. Who could have ever guessed there would be something like that wrapped around a man's stomach inside his shirt?"

Ike-o felt very old, or perhaps as young as when he too had foolishly loved a drunkard. In the gathering dusk and standing at his grave, Charlie Hartwell seemed more real than the cruel little man who lately had lived in Ike-o's mind. The strutter and laugher, the good-timer who walked with his boy's hand on Mechanic Avenue, the old man had been a corker. "He was a pistol, wasn't he, Ma?" Ike-o asked.

"Something went wrong," she said. "He always said it was the times. One time he laid in that bed there and he cried and when I said, 'Charlie, honey, what's wrong?' he said, 'I come on the tail end, Yolanda, I ain't nothing but the horse's tail!' He cried all night, thinking he come from good people and he wasn't amounting to nothing himself."

"I kind of miss him," Ike-o said.

Yolanda wept again. "I'm glad to hear you say that, Isaac," she said. "I'm real glad. After all, we ain't got nothing but each other, you know, the people we live with. I look back on my life with Charlie and maybe I'm a little bit sad, but mostly I'm grateful. You understand, Isaac? — What would I have had without Charlie?" She touched her cheek where bruises had been and a worse pain than that in the skin. "I don't remember nothing but the good," she said. "We had some good times I think, Isaac, and I'm real grateful to your daddy." She wept softly.

"I know what you mean, Ma," he said. "I got plenty of things to be grateful for myself. I ain't been no prize package."

Ike-o found Gedunsky walking slowly and smoking a cigarette on the hill above the railroad yards. There were almost no trains that stopped there any more. The Catfish wore a long raincoat and walked with his head held high as if he inhaled the early evening fragrance.

"It sure is going to be a beautiful night," he said, and asked, "Did you ever notice that the nights never changed in Sobaski's Stairway? — Tonight could be September 1935, or 1917, or 1902. It's the days that make things look different, the nights are the same. Isn't this a beautiful night coming?"

"Like you say, it's all over," Ike-o said. "I thought I had plenty of time, but I guess I don't. I got questions on my mind."

"Go ahead, ask."

"I don't know how to start."

Gedunsky stopped and turned to Ike-o.

"Marry her," he said. "Marry that blonde little Polish girl. Don't ask no questions, marry her." He pulled up his raincoat, making it fit his suitcoat.

"She's a tramp!" Ike-o said quietly. "I ain't marrying

no broad I can't trust. Why are you changing your mind about her suddenly?"

The Catfish threw away his cigarette, shooting it far with his forefinger into the middle of what had been Mechanic Avenue. "Well, *sie gezunt,* as the Spanish say. I wish you the best."

"Don't play me like that, Catfish." The warmth of the night was eluding Ike-o; it slipped away from him in O. C.'s anger. He said, "I thought we were friends, Oscar."

Oscar Gedunsky knew the value of nights filled with lights and warmth and familiarity, and even friendship. "What's the use of me turning into a burglar with you, Isaac?" he asked. "Tell me Dolly Smolcher got bad blood in her veins, but the science books say it doesn't happen that way. Maybe a daughter of royalty she ain't, but me and you ain't neither — I ain't class, I wouldn't know it if I fell over it. I happen to be the son of Simon Gedunsky the tailor, named Oscar for an uncle who died in a cellar in London from the fumes of an old-style washing machine. Do I got the right to tell you Dolly Smolcher ain't got nine lives? Who am I? — If Simon Gedunsky's sad-assed boy had a chance, then so does everybody else. We don't even know where the other Oscar Gedunsky is buried — hah! I should be calling people names, me a cab driver at seventy-two."

"You think Dolly got a chance with the right guy?" Ike-o asked.

"Absolutely," the Catfish said. "Everybody got a chance, once a day, in the morning. See, they're still alive, that's the chance."

The Catfish started to walk again, and it seemed to Ike-o

that the night would last forever: walking along with the Catfish as they had walked a thousand times before, the Catfish nodding and saying "Hello there" to people on the street, their footsteps in the soft, cool night — it could not all be ending. It was too real.

"Hell," Ike-o said, "I'm only twenty-one, I got a lot of good things going to happen to me."

"Marry that broad," the Catfish said. "I ain't saying no more. Don't ask me no more questions." O. C. tapped his white head. "It's up here," he said. "You can't cut out on that. Or this." He prodded with his forefinger Ike-o's chest.

"I ain't in love no more," Ike-o said.

"You're an idealist," the Catfish said. "You're like me, the world don't look right to us no matter how wrong we are."

"It sure ain't a good world."

"Who knows that better than Square-shake, but it's what you make it," the Catfish said. "As long as you're alive there's a chance things will improve. The end is the end. Marry that broad, Isaac, believe me. A person can start a new life every morning; that's the kind of animal we are."

"You make good sense when you ain't lying, Catfish," Ike-o said. "But there ain't no love."

"Okay, frown, sulk, punch somebody in the eye and, after you're done? — Sulk some more. Keep moving, boy, keep moving. That's what life is."

"I didn't say there wasn't gratitude," Ike-o said. "I just meant the old love is gone."

16

Ike-o had not been out toward Fifteenth Street for a few weeks and he was not surprised to see that piece by piece there had been carried away the stairway of the bootlegger Sobaski. Harris' Hill seemed of a lighter brown and bare where the steps had been, but already plants were growing where the wooden steps had once shielded the ground from the sun.

Ike-o went each night for five futile nights out to Emma Carnavan's bus. He stood a short distance away from the bus, surveying the path down which Dolly would come. He waited to make a final payment big enough to release him.

If she were a man it would have been easy. He would have stepped from the brush or better yet waited for a crowd to form on Mechanic and told the other man to put his fists up and then made a few gestures toward fighting and allowed the other man to punch him silly. That would have been all to it. But it was a woman who had loved him and whom he had made foolish: before her friends, her father, her prospective bridegroom, and herself. He owed the debt to Dolly's next marriage. He wanted to make it good, to put her husband in the top position, not somewhere where in the mind of Dolly Smolcher and the rest the poor chump was set up as second choice, runner-up, the receiver of the leavings from Ike-o Hartwell.

Each night he combed his blond hair smooth to keep the short bristles down. The oil made his hair darker but neater. It was important to him to look potent, undeceptive, himself, shoulders wide above the narrow triangle of white T shirt that showed where he missed the top two buttons of his khaki shirt. He wished each night she were a man; he did not know about his feelings afterward — but he was sure that it would be worse than a beating. He knew no other way to repay Dolly for his mistreatment. He sighed and waited.

He had thought at first that there was nothing further to be done. It was over between them, evened out by his beating, which was, among other things, for the years he had foolishly believed he was important because of her affection. He felt she had cheated him; but then in reviewing his life he realized that if she had not given him something to which to hold, there would have been a huge emptiness bounded only by despair and the old brick tenements.

All of Sobaski's Stairway seemed larger because the buildings were absent and only flat, glaring ground remained. He saw Dolly each night of the five coming for her boy, but he waited. He wanted Fats to be a witness and the anonymous bridegroom whom he would make suffer otherwise, just as he had suffered with a sickness about other, invisible men who might have loved Dolly. Here at least would be one head handed the man on a platter. Ike-o walked softly about on the leaf-dappled sod, watching each night the play of shadows and moonlight on the bits of broken bottles that dotted the path to Emma Carnavan's bus. He observed that the grass was as high as a person's ankles now that the stairway was gone. The people who lived in the government housing project on top of Harris' Hill did not come through Sobaski's Stairway. They used feeder roads coming in from another place, Aspen, a neighborhood only slightly less dangerous than Sobaski's Stairway. The grass was not wet until late and made a fine, deep cushion. Probably get bit by a snake, Ike-o thought, and laughed to himself.

He felt like a ghost, standing back and watching the living. He was not in their lives any more, those people who coughed and bobbled around a dirty old bus in a tramp wilderness. He wished for Dolly's sake that he truly loved her. Then it would be real; but the dirt stayed with him, the insinuations of a Mechanic Avenue education and a stomach too full of life even while he ground new experiences in his teeth.

He had tried to love her again, but suspicion was a pervasive virus; it ate at him just when he thought it was gone. He had only to forgive her, to realize that they were two separate people whose paths would never cross again. But that would have made the past useless. It would have meant nothing. If forgiveness meant anything, then Ike-o owed Dolly plenty — she owed him nothing, all the giving was from her. The statue of Jesus had its head again, glued there by Sladic for five dollars, and forgiveness for his father lay good in Ike-o's heart.

Ike-o noticed that no one had come to steal the empty garbage cans. Those that had not been knocked down by wild, raging dogs stood remote where the sidewalks had been and cast shadows on the bricks like proper but rusty tin sundials.

There were two public buildings left standing, the Police Station and a movie theater which had been converted into a Polish church. The marquee still stood in the front (the next attraction nothing) where the congregation had subscribed to have the top of the theater torn off and a steeple built. All of the windows were broken, the glass movie doors picked clean of aluminum and glass. Most of the church's parishioners had moved to other neighborhoods long before the condemnation notice had come from the state. An old woman trudged before the abandoned building. She waved at Ike-o every day but Ike-o avoided her. The old woman wore a picket sign with words Ike-o could not read and she called across the field as he walked, "Pray, soldier, pray for this church." Ike-o walked quickly around her every day.

Then on the sixth night — he knew it would probably be, as it was, a Saturday night — a man walked down the path with Dolly. He was a little man with his shoulders straight, not a young man and not touching Dolly but bringing to Ike-o a feeling like a heaviness on his own neck and shoulders. He had watched her for five nights, thinking only of her as another woman, perhaps even admiring in a detached way her slim beauty. But seeing her with this man brought to him again the knowledge of Dolly as a woman whom he had deeply loved. He remembered her and remembered the times when the memory of her had been the only sweet thing in his life. He closed his eyes, hoping he would not quit. My God, he thought, I'm wondering if she's sleeping with the chump. I'm jealous.

He allowed his body to finish the movement around which it had crouched and coiled while he had waited for six nights. He strode toward the bus. He knocked on the door in the darkness.

There were no faces, only a big debt to be paid, and the debt spoke through Ike-o Hartwell.

"Dolly, don't be a fool," Ike-o said clearly and loud, "this marriage with this man ain't for you. Tell him right now it's off."

"You're crazy. Oh, Ike-o, you're crazy."

The people there stood back from him, as far back as the bus's cramped walls would allow them, as if the insanity of which Dolly spoke might actually erupt into danger. Emma Carnavan held a bread knife.

"You don't love this man," Ike-o said, "you love me."

"You're wrong," Mr. Molyak said, "you are very wrong. If love is what you call it, then it's not enough. Leave us alone, Ike-o."

"You ought to give me a cigar instead of growling at me, old-timer," Ike-o said. "It takes a man from the Animal Rescue League to lead a bitch like that Dolly Smolcher, and I'm the man can do it." He waved his hand toward the bus door. "You don't want to get mixed up with this family," he said, and stopped abruptly as if he were thinking. "I'll give them this though, Pop," he continued, apparently having come to a judicious decision, "there wasn't one of the Smolcher girls wouldn't ask for a pair of bloomers or at least a two-pound box of chocolates before she'd give up her maidenhood for the thousand and second time — excepting the mother, Marg, she liked shoes and caramel crunchies. It ain't me making this up — " Ike-o raised his right hand up as if offering testimony at a trial. "It's history, Pop. Everybody on Mechanic Avenue knew the girls from this family, it's history, like in a book, they ain't too reliable about some things."

Ike-o patted his groin confidently. "I got what Dolly Smolcher wants." He smiled at all of them. "Come on, Dolly, kiss the old man good-by — I'll give him back anything you owe him for any bracelets he bought you or anything." He smiled at all of them again. "I can handle Dolly Smolcher, I always could."

He patted himself again and hitched up his trousers.

"Get out of here," Fats said. He raised his fist.

"Yeah," Ike-o said, and felt Fats' blow, but it was not a fist. Fats had hit him with a flat palm as one strikes an animal or a hysterical person. He fell back toward the bus's door, clutching his face. "You shouldn't have done that, Fats," he said.

There was no mistaking the look in Dolly's eyes; in another moment she would have flown to him, held him, told him, "Don't cry, don't cry, Ike-o." For this was the Ike-o she loved, the defenseless, the dumb brute son of Charlie Hartwell; born in a toilet room, doomed to the dark side of the street.

Ike-o took off his army belt, observing again fear and confusion.

"Tell him good-by," Ike-o said, waving the belt, "tell him good-by or I'll let you have it, Dolly."

"Go home, Ike-o," the little man, the clown, said. Ike-o looked at him closely, apparently angry, but weighing him, and not to fight him but weighing his courage — he stood there three feet away, a full head shorter and too stupid to realize that had Ike-o wanted he could have knocked him to the floor of the bus and trampled him. He was stooped and not young. He was the chump dumb enough to want Dolly with no questions asked.

"You're old, mister," Ike-o said to Mr. Molyak, "and your teeth ain't good." He smiled insultingly at the man with his own brushed teeth. "You're in pretty good shape for an old-timer, but look at this." He rolled up his sleeve. "See that arm," he said, "that's a man's arm, it's going to do plenty before it's done. Ask Dolly what these arms can do." Ike-o strolled the length of the bus and back to the door.

"In five years," he said, "okay, give her ten, that pretty Dolly there is going to be thinking plenty about Isaac Hartwell, at least once a day. You know when, mister? — at night. Listening to you breathing she's going to be getting hot all over and thinking about me, and she's going to be regretting her mistake." Ike-o rejoiced for Dolly's next twenty years when her baby would be a man and she would love her husband and the two of them could always reaffirm their love for each other by going back to their hatred of Ike-o Hartwell.

"You're lousy, kid," Fats said, "there ain't nothing right about you."

The little man did not know what to say; talking was not one of his stronger points. "Go home," he said, "go home, please."

Ike-o tucked his belt in his pants. "Choose," he said. He loved the little man very much; he would still be around, the damned comical clown, when the brooding memories of Sobaski's Stairway were gone. He would be around and not asking questions when the questions of Ike-o Hartwell had disappeared with the bricks of Mechanic Avenue. "Me or him?" Ike-o asked. "You ain't getting another chance, Dolly."

"You better go, Ike-o," Dolly said.

"That's for certain," Fats said.

"I love Dolly," Mr. Molyak said, to Dolly, to Fats, to Emma, and even to Ike-o and anyone else who would ever question him.

"Chump," Ike-o said, but only in play-acting to Dolly, not even in his game able to hurt permanently the decency in the little man's face. For who was he but the receiver of what no one else wanted? He has a round face just like my mother's, Ike-o thought, after he stood alone again on the path. He smiled. He had called them all in the bus a herd of pigs and spat on the floor before he left.

Ike-o stopped on the way home to watch the old woman in her solitary promenade before the abandoned church. The woman wore a picket sign, amateurishly lettered: GOD WILL NOT LET THIS CHURCH BE TORN DOWN. The woman's cheeks trembled.

"My mother and father were married here," she babbled, and fell to her knees chanting a prayer.

Then she looked up at Ike-o, interrupting herself. "If all of you believe in God," she asked, "why is it you do not all pray for miracles?" She closed her eyes, blotting out everything but the massed hypocrites who followed her and goaded her to renewed desperation. Ike-o said good luck, but the woman in man's shoes did not seem to hear.

On the way up Gardenia Street, Ike-o whistled, "I can't give you anything but love, baby." He whistled for the old woman and Mr. Molyak and his mother, for the dummies and the people who were not hep enough to run away from a bad deal. "Hell," he said to himself, "I'm keeping moving." He was amazed. "I'm still alive," he said to an invisible Catfish. "I'm intact, I ain't in pieces."

The morning brought Ike-o Hartwell no pain, only regret, soft and sad; but nevertheless it was morning.